"I"

QUEST FOR
THE
INVISIBLE KEYS

G. Stuart Nakay

Published in 2012 by New Generation Publishing

First Edition

Cover Design and Illustration
Walker Tong

www.newgeneration-publishing.com

 New Generation Publishing

"I"

QUEST FOR THE INVISIBLE KEYS

The story, "I-Quest for the Invisible Keys", is truly unique. "I" is the ultimate journey to find out who we really are. Written in the first person, I, me, myself, the story engages the readers to be somewhat interactive, placing themselves in the role of the main character, the lost child.

None of the major characters in the story have names and there is very little dialogue. The story is told from the child's perspective and is entirely symbolic. The child represents any and all men, women, girls, and boys. Weaknesses and imperfections exposed, the child must meet the challenges, as in life, head on. The story is not so much about "human beings" as it is about "being human."

Life is a constant, never ending struggle we all have to endure while trying to find the correct or comfortable balance that will provide an acceptable level of happiness.

The keys the child must collect are not your ordinary keys. These keys are invisible, intangible, untouchable, but priceless in terms of material wealth. Not easily attained, these keys transcend all cultures, races, and religions, forming an integral part of the foundation for building character and being a better person. These virtues are highly desirable, yet rarely used or incorporated into our daily routines. We opt for the easy way out, this is human nature, and we are all guilty of neglecting these virtues, using them only when we see fit, or suits our purpose.

Influenced by the world around us, these virtues must be taught, practiced, and endeared, becoming part of our lives, benefiting all as well as ourselves. We are all blessed with freedom of choice, so we must choose wisely, spawning success and happiness in our lives.

ONE

The Awakening

WITHOUT WARNING, MY WORLD WENT BLACK. Spinning, swirling, plummeting through the darkness, sucked into the vortex, and hurled across an unknown infinite expanse, I was helpless. Falling, reaching, grappling, kicking, trying desperately to cling onto something, rocketing out of control, I was doomed. My body went limp and I could feel absolutely nothing. THEN IT ALL STOPPED.

I lay motionless, almost afraid to move, not sure if I could move. My legs felt numb. My entire back and the base of my neck and skull were inundated with the painful sensations of small stones or gravel digging into my flesh. Semi conscious, I tried moving my fingers and wiggling my toes. I had little feeling, and my entire being was void of energy. I lay still and waited, hoping to muster some movement from my lifeless body. Slowly, the darkness gave way to the light, and I felt the warmth of the sun caress me. I raised my arm to shield my eyes. One at a time, I began to open them. Adjusting to the light, I lowered my arm.

I found myself, on my back, staring up at the clear blue sky. How long I had been there was anybody's guess. I certainly could not determine any sort of time frame. I watched the thin clouds pass overhead and felt the cool wind buffer the heat. I wiggled my fingers more rapidly, the feeling returning to my limbs, I was alive. I flexed my knees and placed the other hand on my heart, it was still beating. I braced myself, struggling to raise my dead weighted upper body into a sitting position. I was groggy and found it difficult to focus, still staring at the ground around me. I was stunned. Had I fallen from the sky? That's what it felt like, skydiving without a parachute, not too bright. Maybe I had just fallen out of bed? Guess not, where's my house? Where am I?

My eyes began gradually adjusting to the brightness. I blinked and winced, my eyes welling up. I wiped my eyes with my shirt sleeve and looked around. I found myself on a hard-pan roadway, seemingly in the middle of nowhere. I struggled to my knees trying to get some perspective of the area. The wilderness was vast, appearing endless, reaching as far as the eye could see. Tall trees, hills, undulating landscape, wispy knee high grass, and rocky terrain in every direction. I shut my eyes for a second or two, hoping this was merely a dream and it would all disappear, but it did not. I was still here, all alone, at the mercy of the elements and my surroundings. What place was this? Where in God's name was I?

My sense of direction was skewed, not really being able to pinpoint north from south. I could only tell by the sun which rises in the east, that it must be early morning. I set my mental compass for future reference, shaking my head in disbelief. I made another three hundred and sixty degree sweep hoping to see some human movement nearby, or at least hear something familiar. Nothing recognizable, nothing familiar, nobody in sight, I was terrified.

I painfully tried to remember, but had no recollection of how I got here, or why I would even venture into such an area without my friends or family. Where was I and how did I come to be here? These questions and a multitude of others reverberated inside my head, torturing my mind. I found no answers, no reasons, and no logical explanation as to where I was, and why I was here. The only thing I knew for certain being...I WAS LOST AND ALONE.

I felt unusually weak, a momentous effort being required to reach a standing position. I steadied myself and stood in silence waiting for some semblance of strength to return. I staggered over to a large granite stone and leaned against its warm surface. I was confused, disoriented, and frightened. My legs were still weak and my stomach felt especially empty. My throat was parched and my lips dry from the exposure to the sun. How long had I been lying there? Where was my family? Why hadn't anyone found me? Where had I been, or what had happened just before? I did not understand any of this. It did not make any sense at all.

I honestly could not remember anything I could associate with being here, absolutely no connection, but I was here, where ever "here" was. Impossible I thought, absolutely impossible.

I felt abandon. Everything familiar to me, was gone. My emotions were beginning to get the best of me. After all, what was an eleven-year old child doing here, in this place of all places, completely alone, inconceivable? The longer I pondered all the possibilities, the more frustrated and upset I became. Looking again out into the vast unknown, a quiet fear started to set in.

What or who was out there? I could only hope a friendly face would turn up soon and take me out of here. Wishful thinking I guess, but my only source of hope for now. The place was draped in silence as if every living creature must have stopped to take a look. The eyes of the forest were watching. I was sure. They could see me, but I could not see them. I began to feel uncomfortable and nervous. Fear of the unknown is the worst fear of all, but I could not let it defeat me, not yet anyway. I tried to suck it up, stay strong, and see the situation for what it really was, a bunch of trees, hills, and grass. Not that scary. The being alone part was the tough one.

Independent by nature, I enjoyed my freedom with confidence, but was never left alone like this. Surely this was some sort of mistake, some friends playing a trick on me, must be. Maybe a deranged game of hide and seek, testing my mettle to the max. No way, none of my friends would be caught dead in a place like this. I thought it wise to move around, walk a little to stimulate my circulation. I dragged my heavy legs a little ways down the narrow roadway, cupped my hands to my mouth, and shouted at the top of my lungs.

"Help!"

I began to cough violently, as the dryness in my throat restricted my attempt. I cleared my airway, spit the dust and dryness from my mouth, and strained to create some lubricating saliva. I took a minute or two and then another try.

"Help...help...anyone...is anyone out there...help!"

I screamed for several minutes until my vocal chords were hoarse. My appeal echoed through the hills and tall trees, with no immediate response. It was apparent I could yell all day and all night with the same result, nothing. There was no one here, at least not now. I was truly alone and pretty much helpless.

I looked to the sky for a heavenly answer, but only saw what I thought to be a large bird circling high overhead. A vulture in wait perhaps. Hope not waiting for me. I could hear my heart thumping, the uncertainty creating anxiety. I envisioned an eagle waiting for its chance to dive-bomb me and mercilessly gouge my eyes out. Boy, what a thought. My imagination was getting the better of me.

I watched for a while as the bird came in for a closer look. Velvety blue with a Mohawk hairdo, the inquisitive blue jay seemed to be on friendly terms with me and this foreign hinterland. I had never really seen a blue jay before, quite regal and larger than I would have thought. I was relieved. The bird soared higher, disappearing amongst the branches of a tall evergreen. I lumbered back to the granite stone, even more exhausted and frustrated than before. Sitting on one of its smoother protrusions, I pondered the possibilities. What to do? Sit and wait? Keep screaming? Pray for a miracle? No choice. Exploring the territory could be dangerous. Better to starve to death than be eaten alive by the predators of the forest. Better safe than sorry. I decided to stay put for the time being, and keep thinking about my very limited options.

After an hour or so, the stress and the pressure were beginning to take its toll. My mind and body were weary and my eyelids drooping. Too much thinking without resolution...so demoralizing and upsetting. No doubt I was severely traumatized and fatigued, very sleepy, but I could not let myself fall asleep now in case someone or something passed nearby. Perhaps a plane, a helicopter, a search and rescue team, may be looking for me at this very moment. I had to stay positive, and on guard, surely I would be found. I could not chance missing any opportunity to be emancipated from this troubling ordeal. I must stay observant and pay close attention to my line of sight. I must listen to the sounds as I may hear something familiar, some sound that could be important, a sound that could ultimately save my life. My senses were the only tools at my disposal, and I had to employ them full bore, continually maintaining a high alert status. It was my only chance.

Watching the sun continue its ascent, I realized the hours were passing quickly and nothing had changed. The silence was my only companion. For a city boy, this was just too peaceful, too tranquil, too lonely, way too unnerving. The wind whispered through the treetops and the cumulus clouds passed slowly by in the distance. I tried to make shapes out of the clouds, a game we played on family picnics in my younger days. The novelty however had long worn off, and the time waster lasted only a few minutes. No more games, I had to figure my way out of this, if there was one?

I tried to concentrate on the present, but the difficulty of not knowing why or how, was eating away at me. I don't believe I had ever truly been scared or frightened before, but I was getting there now and getting there fast. I had always had someone around me or least near me, never this feeling of being so alone, isolated, and lifeless. The mere thought of being left alone, out here, to an ill fated demise, was tearing me up inside.

There was no way this was possible. How could this happen? Why did this happen? What did I do to deserve this? I kept asking myself questions and receiving no answers, or none that I wanted to hear. This must be some kind of punishment. Maybe I did something terrible in my last life, or maybe this was just fate.

I remember a teacher saying the day we are born, our entire life has already been planned, organized, and finalized. Nothing we can do to change it. I sure hoped the teacher was wrong because I was not keen on dying out here all alone. My thoughts were becoming increasingly negative and detrimental, but I could not stop. There was nothing positive coming to mind, no saving grace, at least I could not see it. The circumstances were dire and I was in serious trouble. Those were the facts. Baffled, I held my head in my hands, my despair unquestionable, and then...I HEARD A SOUND.

TWO

The Voice

I ABRUPTLY STOOD, frantically searching in all directions for the source. It was definitely not the birds, and not the wind. Faint and haunting would be the best description, but where was it coming from. I started jogging around the immediate area shouting again and again as loud as I could. The sound was still there, like mumbling, murmuring, muttering, but from where? Animals do not make these kinds of sounds. My hope rekindled, I searched in earnest but to no avail. I threw my hands into the air. "Where are you? Why can't I see you? Come out, come out, where ever you are?"

Maybe it was nothing? Maybe my mind playing tricks on me? Maybe the onset of insanity? Maybe all of the above? What a nightmare. I was just spinning my wheels, becoming more anxious, and annoyed, so I stopped. I was starting to hyperventilate so took a few deep breaths in an attempt to regain my composure. I focused and listened carefully. I had to find out where the sound was coming from. I stood silent and motionless, trying to void my mind of all other thoughts, concentrating only on the sound.

I knew the sound must be nearby for me to hear it, so I must be patient and wait. I closed my eyes and tried to relax. Placing myself in a state of semi meditation, I decided to let the sound come to me.

"Where are you?" I asked calmly.

"Where can I find you? Who are you? You have found me. I need to see you, and I need your help. I am waiting."

The faint oration was now becoming more audible. Closer and closer, louder and louder, finally I heard the

Voice. The sound was not coming from outside, or around me. I placed my hands over my ears shutting out any possible distracting noise. The sound was trapped inside my head. I could hear it in there. Again I concentrated as hard as I could, and then I heard everything. Like a long distance phone call, the ongoing message was becoming clear, crystal clear. I listened intently to what the Voice had to say.

The revelation was not only surprising, but shocking. I began to tremble. The Voice continued its lengthy narration, than abruptly stopped. I tried to replay the message over in my mind, memorizing every single word, desperately trying to grasp its meaning. I was mesmerized and gazed out into the wilderness. I was speechless, but in the end, realized what I must do. I must listen to the Voice and follow its specific instructions. I laboured to recall the exact words, but eventually succeeded. The words left an indelible mark somewhere in the deep recesses of my brain, and now I could not get them out of my head. Like a catchy advert jingle, I knew the words would be with me forever. The haunting Voice sounded once again, repeating the words one last time.

"Child, you are indeed lost and alone. However, there is hope you will find your way home. How long it takes, is up to you. Regretfully, it is also possible, you may never find your way home, and remain lost forever."

"You must travel the path which lies before you. Along the way you may encounter many challenges, meet many people, and have to make difficult decisions. Your progress may be impeded by many obstacles, physical, mental, and emotional. You must be vigilant and constantly alert. Reality is sometimes confusing. When one thing appears innocent, it may in reality, cause great harm.

When something appears too easy, it may present great difficulty. Be prepared in both mind and body for all your weaknesses will be exposed. Be careful, as danger lurks in many forms, especially when and where you least expect it. You will be challenged at every turn, so expect the unexpected. The outcome is in your hands. You are the master of your destiny."

"Success is never guaranteed, however if successful, you will be awarded with a *key*, a truly unique and valuable *key*. You will need to secure *10 keys, and only then will you find your way.* Go forth and seek what you hope to find. Your odyssey is about to begin...go...GO NOW!"

The Voice vanished, and I looked around quickly to see if I had been mistaken. Was this some kind of illusion? I don't remember having taken any kind of medication, so this was not some hallucination. I hoped and prayed someone was really out there, but the answer to this sixty-four million dollar question was always the same...no one. Now I believe the Voice was truly inside my head. How could it be? What could it be? Who could it be? Could it be the voice of God, or just my conscience playing more mind games. I hoped this was not a game because I was not in the mood for any nonsense. I kept pinching myself, biting my lip, and punching my thigh. Definitely not a game, I sensed something serious was about to take place, and I was smack in the middle of it. An uneasy feeling lingered all around and I became increasingly nervous and jittery.

I had no idea what the Voice meant by *keys*. What kind of keys? No clue. I know what a key is, so I'm sure I'll recognize it when I see it. Now becoming obviously apparent, there was only one way to find out, but I would not find anything standing around here. In the distance, I saw the faint but prominent outline of a narrow pathway winding through the tall thin grass and leading down the hillside. The Voice said I must follow the path that lies before me. That hair line fracture of a trail was the only path I could see, so I presumed it to be the path in question. Hopefully, I had presumed correctly, otherwise the Voice said I may never find my way. I didn't want to hear that, who would?

I took a deep breath. Without food, water, or weapons, I felt weak, defenseless, and at the mercy of my predicament. I had nothing, and only one choice, so I began my trek towards the weather beaten track. I could only hope the path would guide me on my quest to find the keys, and ultimately, my way home. I had no inkling as to where I was going or what may happen along the way. My journey was about to begin without indication as to when or how it would end. The great unknown awaits, time to roll the dice and hope it's not snake eyes.

THREE

The Bridge

AFTER ABOUT THIRTY MINUTES OF HARD MARCHING, I finally reached the distinctive trail which I had seen from a distance. It looked different up close. The grass was worn completely away leaving the dirt exposed. It appeared to go on forever, as far as I could see. The path was the only friend I had to rely on, and I hoped this friend would not disappoint me. I set off through the gently rolling, tree lined valley. I tried to pass the time by whistling some familiar tunes, but that just dried out my already parched throat. And besides, I didn't really know that many tunes. What I wouldn't give for a burger and an ice cold cola. No use thinking about that, it just made things worse. I had to pay attention to my surroundings and be alert. That is what the Voice told me to do. I better listen. I had no conception of what creatures may use the trees as cover, before they attack. I had no way to defend myself, so I would be at their mercy, an easy meal. I was hoping no bears, cougars, or other carnivorous creatures were lurking in the shadows and tall grass. I must remain forever watchful, my life depended on it.

Although hopeful of confronting something more human in form, I quickly realized that may not necessarily negate the danger. On second thought, this area could be home to gangs, bands of thieves, werewolves, yes I believe, or some sort of inbred backwoods cannibals. Who knew who or what really inhabited these lands. I was at a great disadvantage not being privy to my exact location. I could only wonder "what" and "if", not an enviable position for anyone, even an adventurous soul.

Further ahead, the trail widened and turned towards the tree line. I was apprehensive about entering the forested area, but it appeared I had no choice in the matter. The path led in that particular direction, so I must follow, according to the Voice. I stopped at the entry point and trotted along the edge looking for some smooth stones and a walking stick. A little something for protection...better than nothing. I found what I needed in short order and was ready to proceed, with caution.

Entering the shadowy world, the sounds of the forest were all around, initially having a soothing effect. The sun was partially blocked by the tall trees, yet streamed through like golden spears to provide more than enough visibility. Like a nice walk in the park, I began to enjoy it, telling myself I was in no danger, the city was nearby. I stepped on a dry branch and the loud CRACK startled me, bringing me back to earth. Now I was spooked. My legs weary, I began to labour under the strain of no food, rest, or water. I stopped and sat on a fallen tree, to catch my second wind. I began to feel sorry for myself, my weaknesses starting to show through. This was not the time, I had to think help was just around the corner, stay positive. I sat for a while trying to regain my composure, I had to stay calm. Nerves and tension are the foundation of bad decisions. Just like exam day when the night before, a couple computer games interrupted your study time, so you were doomed to failure. Sitting there a bundle of nerves, and choosing all the wrong multiple choice answers, your only hope, the twenty-five percent chance of being correct. Thank God for multiple choices. Honestly, it didn't help, suffered through it more than once, and bombed out every time. Thanks for the memories. I stood up, flexed my arms and legs, and continued my march into Never Neverland.

I calculated I had been walking for several hours and was really running on empty. Up ahead I began to see more light as the trees thinned out significantly. I was hopeful my forest adventure was about to end.

I stepped out of the shadows and into the sun. A large clearing was now in full view, but the sun was going down. There was no way I was going any further in the dark. I would rest here for the night. I found an appropriate resting place, a large clump of soft sod. I thought it a good mattress, so gave it a try. My tired muscles thanked me for the much needed break, and I began to relax. Somewhere in the distance I heard a very familiar, soothing sound, the sound of water. The sound helped calm my mind and I fell asleep.

Morning came quickly. I awoke with the birds chirping and the sun rising over the hilltop. I did not want to move, having found my comfort zone so to speak, but I had to. I stood up stretching, trying to loosen my muscles. I rubbed my eyes and looked around for anything that could be construed as food. My stomach was rumbling like a locomotive rattling over a wooden trestle. What a horrible feeling. Never experienced that one before, hunger, I hate it. I eyeballed the surrounding forestation hoping to spot something edible.

Luckily, I saw something familiar, small pods hanging from a little tree. Closer examination revealed walnuts. Not exactly bacon and eggs, but considering where I was, better than nothing. I gathered some and used two large rocks to crack them open. I chewed with zest as I was starving. After a few walnuts, the nutty mixture was getting stuck in my throat. I needed some liquid, anything. I searched along tree line and spotted some broad leafed ferns. The fresh morning dew had not yet evaporated, so I carefully folded the leaves into a funnel shape, knelt down, and drank an once or two of precious liquid. I found a few more leaves and did the same. At last, some nourishment. No idea how much dirt or how many bugs went down with the precious nectar, but I felt much better. I loaded my pockets with walnuts and was ready to rock. Time to press onward.

I followed the pathway over a small rise and could not believe my eyes.

Directly in front of me was a massive gorge straddled by a *bridge*...of sorts. I moved in for a closer peek. Quite a scenic view...rather breath taking. I estimated a thousand feet to the bottom of the abyss, where a raging river carved its signature through the floor of the canyon.

There was no apparent way around the obstacle. The bridge appeared to be the only conveyance. The river seemed endless and the steep cliffs were not negotiable. There was no path leading anywhere else, only this one way artery over the bridge. This was a dead end, and I mean dead.

The river which provided last evening's soothing lullaby, now presented a potential life and death situation. The quarter mile gap might as well have been twenty miles, as the bridge seemed to be suspended in mid air without any visible signs of support. The rope cables were tattered and frayed, and the wooden planks were rotten and broken. The structure was flimsy and could have been a hundred years old. Who would use it? Who built it? Maybe a century ago this area was home to someone, but not now. This little suspension bridge had the words, "the end" written all over it. The end for anyone who dared cross it.

I jostled with the jute railings and the entire bridge swayed back and forth like a giant sea serpent. It appeared, any weight whatsoever would take this elongated gangplank and its occupants to the riverbed below. I was afraid of heights, and the prospect of having to cross this poor excuse for a bridge was horrifying. Did I really need to cross this impossible, impassible, quarter mile piece of hell, by navigating a structure held together with cobwebs and rusty nails? I would die for sure. No one would ever find my body. What was I going to do now?

I was in no rush to continue and spent the next twenty minutes talking to myself, praying for an answer, one that I wanted to hear. I could see the path continue on the other side, so I must cross, but how? Now would be a good time to come up with a brilliant idea. I did not have one. Levitation came to mind, then the thought of my super power abandoning me in the middle of the cross over brought me quickly back to the challenge at hand. Get real, this was no magic show. I stepped closer to the menacing entrance of the terrifying catwalk, paying close attention to the ropes and the floorboards. I contemplated the margin for error...there wasn't any. I had to get the weight ratio and balance quotient correct. One wrong move and I would be history. I thought I could straddle my walking stick horizontally atop the rope railings the width of the bridge, approximately one metre. I would push the stick forward coordinating my steps in an effort to control the swaying.

No idea if this would work, but it was the only idea I had at the time. Now I needed to talk myself into taking the first step...maybe my last step.

I took several deep breaths and now it was time to put my plan into action. I had to try to distribute my weight evenly with every motion. Here goes. The first few steps offered some hope, so I continued. I tried not to look down or be hypnotized by the sound of the river below. I focused straight ahead looking for weaknesses in the structure and avoiding them if possible. About twenty metres out, I started to feel uncomfortable because up ahead were many broken and damaged footings.

A treacherous undertaking to be sure. I thought of turning back, but looking behind me revealed the footings now broken and splintered, not capable of sustaining any weight. No use thinking about going back. The path lay ahead. I took a few moments to prepare myself mentally, than I took a few more.

I knew extra caution was required, and I had a long way to go. I stepped gingerly from board to board, gliding my guide stick across the tops of the rails. The entire bridge would bob up and down from time to time depending on the pressure I exerted. I had to try and control the movement of the structure to enhance my chance of surviving the trip. One wrong move and it could be all over.

My confidence was building with every step as I seemed to guess correctly on where to place my feet. I proceeded slowly, fully aware of the danger. Then it happened. A gust of wind lifted the floorboard in front of me and I took an awkward step.

My foot hit a rotted part of the board and went right through. I was down on one knee, totally off balance, hanging onto my stick for dear life. I struggled to maintain my equilibrium. I turned sideways grasping in terror, granted a bird's eye view of what lay in store for me at the bottom of the canyon. A multitude of jagged rocks and a watery grave lay in wait, thirsting to taste my blood. Not a vision for the weak of heart. I battled my way back, balanced myself, and managed to lift myself out of the hole. I crossed to the next plank which was solid. I was safe, for the moment, if you could call that safe. More like stuck in hell without a fire extinguisher.

My heart was palpitating like the pistons in a sports car. I steadied myself, taking a breather. Calming down a little, I carefully began to move forward. I was nearing the middle of the bridge, the point of no return. No turning back now, I was half way home, figuratively speaking. Maybe half way to the grave was more apropos. Like a turtle in slow motion, I utilized small deliberate steps. I now had my second wind and a regained confidence until I felt the breeze in my face. A few minutes later, I could feel the wind really picking up. The gusts were coming one after the other. I looked skyward as the heavens darkened and I saw a flash in the distance out of the corner of my eye. This was bad news, a storm approaching. The rumble of thunder could be heard, and I began to feel drops of rain. I didn't need this, not now, not ever.

Soon the sky turned a sooty charcoal colour, and I had no light except for the sheet lightning that pierced the cloud cover. I could feel it coming. The thunder clouds unleashed their fury, and the rain pelted down, bouncing off the flooring like hailstones. Now the footing was even more treacherous, slippery, like an ice rink. The large heavy droplets stung my head and face, drenching me within a minute. This was a disaster in the making. I had to think quick before the wind and rain ended my journey, ended my life.

I held onto the staff and knelt down. I thought I could keep a lower centre of gravity by crawling along the pylons. I was hoping to negate the slip factor as well, but knees slide too. The balancing act became more intricate. I wobbled back and forth like a high wire circus performer, only I didn't have a net to fall into, only a canyon waiting to swallow me up when given the opportunity.

The bridge was now swaying in an unpredictable pattern, the darkness and driving rain making it almost impossible to see where I was going. I could not even see the other side. I had never heard such loud and intimidating thunder, it made me cower. The lightning strikes were hitting their targets all around the area. I could hear explosions behind and in front of me along with the sound of falling trees. I could only hope the lightning would keep missing this target, but it might be only a matter of time.

The bridge was now twisting and turning, out of control. I had to get off the bridge as soon as possible. The structure was on life support, and unfortunately, I needed it to survive. I was hanging on with all my strength and trying to crawl at the same time. I was exhausted and had no idea how far I had to go. I was beginning to slide back and forth, the wind throwing me around like a rag doll. The floorboards were cracking and breaking into pieces, and I felt the ropes may come unhinged sending me over the edge. A violent twist to the right caught me completely by surprise and my staff flipped out of my hands and sailed down into the yawning crevasse. My stash of walnuts were squeezed from my pockets, and along with my arsenal of smooth stones, disappeared into the black canyon below. I grabbed the railing with both hands trying to steady myself. What a battle, God help me. I felt at any time, the wind could just pick me up and catapult me into the ravine.

A flash illuminated the other side, and I could see I had but twenty metres to go. I was not sure I could make it because the bridge could be blown away without warning. I slid along the soaked planks, on my knees, my hands now holding onto either side of the damaged rope rails. I was inching closer, but the rain in my face hampered my view and ability to balance. It was impossible to gauge how I would make my great escape, if fortunate enough to negotiate the final ten metres. My chances were two, slim and none. What a calamity. Mother Nature was throwing everything she had at me, but I was determined to fight...fight for my life. I was too close to throw in the towel. I would never give up, not now. I inched forward, lightning strikes all around me, the thunder right on top of me.

A bolt from heaven lit up the sky and I heard an ear splitting crash behind me. I looked back to see a fallen fiery obelisk topple onto the bridge, setting it ablaze. The flames followed the planks like an oil slick. How could this happen? The foot boards were soaking wet. The wall of fire chased after me, and it was catching up quickly. Soon the ropes would burn through and the bridge would collapse. I only had a few steps to go. I staggered trying to stand, holding on tightly to the rails. Suddenly...the unthinkable.

The fire had done its job. The support cables at the far end of the bridge had burned through. I knew this would happen, so held on with all my might as the bridge gave way.

The bridge, now a giant trellis, accelerated towards the rocky cliff. A jarring thud bounced me once with authority into the wall of granite, then another two for good measure. I hung on with all I had left, hoping the bridge would survive its eminent peril.

I was now face first against the cliff, hanging on for dear life. I hoped this end of the bridge would remain secure long enough for me to make my escape. Harry Houdini, where are you when I need you? I pulled myself upwards. Using the bridge as a ladder, I dug in my toes and propelled myself forward. I reached the edge of the cliff just as the fire was about to overtake me. I quickly climbed onto the edge of the precipice and rolled to safety. The entire bridge was now engulfed in flames. I watched in horror as it disintegrated and the lengthy mass of fire lit up the pitch black abyss as it careened down the side of the rugged canyon wall.

The rain and wind continued, but I felt nothing. I lay flat on my back, completely devoid of energy. I was alive and that in itself was hard to believe. I survived and prayed this was the end of the journey.

I crawled away from the edge and leaned against a tree. I was exhausted and my nerves were shot. What a harrowing experience. An hour passed and the weather had taken a turn for the better. The dark clouds sailed off into the distance, the rain and wind subsided. The sun began to peek out from behind the tall trees and the forest had once again become a peaceful place.

I smiled knowing I was safe, and took a seat on large tree stump facing the gaping canyon where the bridge once was. I shook my head in disbelief and closed my eyes. Within seconds an earthy rumble sparked my attention. The whole area was shaking. I dared not move. Was this an earthquake? What next? Are you kidding me? I watched in horror as the other side of the canyon began to move directly toward me. The entire side moving steadily, I could not believe my eyes. Closer and closer it came and finally cementing itself against the near side with tremendous crash. The sheer force knocked me to the ground. The canyon was gone, not a trace, like it had never been there. The scene was like something out of the Bible, with the Red Sea closing in on the Egyptians, who were chasing the Israelites, escaping to the Promised Land.

This was not possible, but I had seen it happen. An immense canyon, taking millions of years to form, and vanishing right before my very eyes. No one would believe this. I was stunned into absolute silence and could not get the image out of my mind. The sound, the grinding, the movement...than nothing.

Still soaking wet, I was counting on the warmth of

the sun to dry me off. I was famished and could see the same walnut tree I had raided in the morning. It had barely survived the ordeal. Many of its branches were broken and most of the nuts were scattered on the ground.

I cracked open a few and found ample water on the leaves of the nearby foliage. I rested for a while and then stood to get my bearings. The path was there, right behind me, beckoning me to follow. It was late, and I decided to conserve what strength I had left and stay here for the night. The area I had rested the night before was now available, so I would sleep there again once the sun had dried it out. I sat on a fallen tree, still astonished and overwhelmed by the day's events.

My mind began to drift, wandering back, back to the second grade. I recalled a time I now remember so clearly for some reason. That afternoon, at recess period, the school bully and his band of followers decided to have some fun, with me.

Not sure why they chose me, but it really didn't matter, someone different every day. Guess it was my turn. I was sitting outside in the school yard eating my recess snack along with one of my school mates. Both of us noticed the gang coming in our direction and decided to hide our head in our food, pretending to talk to each other, hoping they would pass by, but they didn't.

Stopping beside us, the school bully known as "Mason the Monster", pretended to trip over my foot, like I did it on purpose. The jolt knocked my snack to the ground and Mason began mouthing off. He grabbed me by the arm and stood me up, bumping into me, and trying to intimidate me, doing a good job of it to. He starting pushing me and I said nothing. He tried to goat me into saying anything that would give him an excuse to punch me, hit me, or hurt me. My schoolmate Tyler, witnessed the entire event and then to my surprise, stood up, and confronted Mason, telling him to grow up and leave everyone alone.

Mason shifted his attention to Tyler, got right in his face, but Tyler didn't budge. Mason was just about to become aggressive when the buzzer signaled the end of recess. Mason brushed by Tyler mumbling something. We all headed back to class. I never said a word.

Nearing the end of lunch hour, I happened to pass by the side of the school when I heard a commotion. I rounded and corner and saw Mason, his gang, along with many other schoolmates. I could not really see what was going on, so gently threaded my way to a better vantage point.

Mason had Tyler pinned against the wall, pushing him and smashing him up against the brick siding. Mason's group stood lookout for patrolling teachers while Mason stuck his hand in Tyler's face. All the other boys stood and watched. I pushed my way to the front and watched as well.

Some of the others started laughing as the much larger Mason seemed to be toying with Tyler, waiting for Tyler to fight back so he would have an excuse to administer his own brand of school yard justice. I stood there silent, afraid to make a move or utter an objection. Mason finished with Tyler, left him crying, and they all laughed as they walked away. The crowd thinned, no one dared summon the teachers, and I walked away as well, leaving Tyler there to sooth himself. He looked over at me. I looked away and strode off.

Tyler had stuck up for me at recess, but when I needed the courage to return the favour, I could find none. At the time I never even thought about getting involved. Why should I suffer the wrath of Mason the Monster, it wasn't worth it. I wished I could redeem myself for my lack of valour, but it was too late. Tyler and I didn't really meet much anymore after that. I couldn't blame him, but at the time I honestly didn't care, no great loss I thought. Just another day at school.

The loud CRACK of a splitting tree finally giving in to the forces of nature brought me back to the present, and then I heard a familiar sound. The sound I could not get out of my head, the Voice.

"COURAGE, also known as FORTITUDE, is the ability to confront fear in the face of pain, danger, uncertainty or intimidation. Physical Courage allows one to cope with physical pain, hardship, and threat of death.

Moral Courage allows one to prevail in the face of shame, scandal, and discouragement. Courage is the ability to handle any situation with courageous energy. Courage requires you give 100% every time you seek to accomplish anything. Not do so, lacks real courage. Courage is to face all life's challenges with a resolute and moral heart. Courage and bravery are not to be confused, yet both are necessary to achieve life's goals.

To engage in a seemingly hopeless battle and not give up, is courageous. It is also courage to bear life's hardships without complaining, and maintain composure under adverse circumstances, approaching good and bad times in life with equal composure, dignity, and patience."

The Voice then faded into oblivion, gone as quickly as it had come. What was that all about? I needed help, not a bunch of rambling gibberish. Get me out of here, that's what I want. The Voice's dialogue sounded like something I heard once in bible study class. I forgot all the quotes from scripture, falling asleep during most the lessons, so boring. I only really remember one because I thought it sounded cool. Psalm 23 I believe.

"I walk through the shadow of the valley of death,

yet I fear no evil, for thou are with me."

Yeah, I like that one. Maybe the Voice was trying to tell me the same thing, only I think he used too many extra words. It did not matter anyways. I was still here in the middle of a whopping mess. I really was hoping this was the end, but I had a terrible feeling this was only the beginning. Tomorrow would come too soon, and I must again travel the path that lay before me. Hopefully, I will awake with more answers than questions because I have a funny feeling I am going to need an awful lot more answers if this goes on any longer.

FOUR

The Village

EVERY MUSCLE IN MY BODY ached as I rose from my grassy bed. I tried some simple calisthenics to loosen up before venturing off. Painful was the best way to explain it, absolutely painful. Felt like I had been run over by a steamroller, whatever that feels like. Sore and stiff, with no one to listen to my complaining, I began duplicating my culinary routine from yesterday. Walnuts and leaf dew, better than nothing, yum...yum. Once again, I loaded my pockets with walnuts. Never know when or where the next meal will come from. The path beckoned me, and I was eager to follow. I gathered in my new found courage and was off to the races. For some reason I felt today just may be my lucky day. Yeah I know...don't count on it!

The trail carved its way through some light forestation and then into open pasture. The setting was serene, no strange sounds to speak of, definitely hitting my comfort zone. I shifted into cruise control, not wavering from the path. Like a little robot train, I just stayed on the track. A loud "CRACK" came from the tree line and I saw something race through the tall grass. I stopped and stay motionless, waiting to see what would emerge from the cover. I could see the branches move and I hoped whatever emerged was smaller than me. Several metres in front of me, the animal dashed into view. I jumped back. A baby deer, a fawn paraded proudly past, not paying me any notice whatsoever. So innocent...so unaware...so beautiful. I wanted to take it with me, my new best friend. The fawn stopped briefly to take a good look around then scurried off through the field, so I continued on.

After several hours, the path took a gradual turn and headed into the forest again. I really did not want to enter. I was really starting to hate all this in and out of the woods, but had no choice as this is where the path led me. I have to admit, I was getting used to the shadows and eerie quiet. After yesterday's adventure on the bridge, I was confident I could handle a few tall trees and a bunch of cast off shadows.

Hour after hour, I trudged along the pathway, resting from time to time, and nibbling a walnut or two. I was not afraid in the least, although many crazy thoughts crossed my mind. Was the area inhabited by headhunters, cannibals, or insane forest people, possibly more dangerous than any four legged creatures? Bigfoot, Sasquatch, Aliens...man was I getting carried away. I gave my head a shake and ordered myself to pay attention, focus. Difficult to block out everything, but I tried. Up ahead, the forest began to thin out once more and I exited the trees and arrived at another open area. The trail seemed endless. Where was it taking me? The million dollar question had no immediate answer. Looking off to the side, I noticed a familiar shape. A small hut type structure was camouflaged by the lingering shadows.

I began to get excited. Human contact must be close at hand. Somebody must live there or use this shed for something, possibly a hunter. Hoping the little shelter was not a place for bodily fluid relief, an outhouse, I pushed my way through the low lying branches and foliage finally reaching the hut.

I called out, but no response. I walked around looking for footsteps, an indicator of current use, nothing. I imagined someone stepping out to greet me, but was not the case. If vacant, I hoped I could find something useful inside as I had no tools or weapons. I gently grabbed the handle and slowly opened the door.

I just about came out of my skin as a small raccoon darted to freedom. What a fright. I carefully peered in hoping not to find anything larger and meaner inside. The coast was clear, really clear. I entered and found the tiny shed completely empty, except for a few logs, a lot of dust, and a musty smell. Along one side of the ceiling was a ledge. I backed up a pace or two and spotted a stick, or maybe a pole. I hoisted myself upwards, lunging forward, grabbing the object. Only a minute needed to scour the remaining square footage, nothing more to see, empty.

I brought the staff outside and used a fern leaf to wipe away the excess dust. I had stumbled upon the most beautiful piece of hickory, an excellent walking stick. I almost hated to leave the hut as it would provide protection and shelter against bad weather.

Possibly a visitor would show up soon because someone had to know about this shack. Wishful thinking once again on my part. Could be months before anyone lay claim to the shed. I could not depend on anyone finding me. I must follow the path and find the way, so I thought it best to keep moving.

A short time later, the forest rapidly thinned and I was met by a bank of low lying clouds. I could see the path at my feet, but that was about all. The fog was thick, hiding anything and everything beyond. I just followed the path. I thought that the safest move. Light began to penetrate the haze and soon it vanished revealing a wall of rippled heat. I stopped immediately. This must be some sort of illusion due to my exhaustion or possibly the cause and effect of some weird refraction of light. From the other side, I could hear faint sounds in the distance, but impossible to form any type of visualization. The path led right through it, so I proceeded with caution.

31

Passing through only took a matter of seconds then I jogged up and over a small incline spotting something up ahead. I detected movement, possibly people, animals, or both. I quickened my pace as I desperately wanted to reach the location. Now within a couple hundred metres, I stopped and smiled. Before me was some kind of village or nomadic encampment. I saw people and farm animals, horses and goats. There was a caravan of colourful wagons scattered about, and the place seemed to be beaming with activity. The scene reminded me of a gypsy camp or possibly they were a band of entertainers from a travelling circus. It did not matter, what mattered was I would finally have some human contact, and help. It's about time, and thank you. I saluted the heavens and proceeded with zest.

I sauntered into the camp and nonchalantly strolled down the main drag. I observed all the people and all the action. Then I noticed something quite peculiar. I was obviously an outsider, yet no one in the village seemed to notice me at all, like I was invisible. I kept walking and looking, taking in all the sights. The main strip was plastered with vendors and farther up the street, furriers and animal handlers. Jugglers, fire eaters, and contortionists were practicing their handiwork, and I marveled at the abilities of these performers. I thought this village was an amazing place, and greatly enjoyed the free show. So much activity in the middle of nowhere...but why? Must be something going on here! I believed these folks must be a friendly, helpful bunch, and my confidence in finding help peaked.

I decided to select a suitable candidate, someone easy to speak to. I looked for a woman with a kind face, must be a motherly thing. After several minutes I sighted a woman with a small boy. I was certain she would be sympathetic and assist me. What mother would refuse to help a child?

I approached and began to speak. She completely ignored me. I positioned myself directly in front of her and spoke. She looked at me, smiled politely and said nothing. It was as if she could not understand a single word I was saying. She took her child by the hand and walked away.

Maybe she was deaf, or possibly did not speak English. I thought it best to try another, so again I attempted to select another suitable subject. I tried a grandma and a young man tending his horses. The result was the same.

No one here could, or wanted to communicate with me. Listening carefully, I tried to determine the language these people were speaking but could not. Obviously foreign, possibly European, or even maybe some enigmatic, archaic dialect. This was a big problem. How could I talk to them? Everyone seemed aloof and uncaring, lost in their own little world. The setting appeared truly surreal, but it was real, I was here in the present. How could all these people look at me and not see me? I kept asking myself this question. There must be a way, some method I could use to communicate with them. These people were not from outer space, they were human, just like me. Think...think I kept telling myself.

Then I had an idea. Maybe I should try a child, a kid. After all, kids understand kids. That was the case, where I came from anyways. I was hoping it was the same wherever these kids came from. I knew I could communicate with some kids, so I scoured the settlement. Within a few minutes, I noted a young boy walking by himself up the centre of the main thoroughfare. Not sure where he was going, but he looked normal enough and hopefully could help. I watched for a moment, and soon another group of four young boys quickly caught up and seemed to be following my target. I had a feeling something bad was going to happen. I thought I best keep my distance, but continued to keep tabs.

The group moved closer and closer. I thought they were preparing for an attack, but no, they had something else in mind. The group slowed, and the boy I had noted, stopped in front of a fruit stand. He began to examine the fruit, selecting some pieces to buy, or so I thought.

The vendor came to meet him at the far end of the stand. At that precise moment, the group of boys raided the stall, quickly filling a sack and then turning over one of the carts, blocking the vendor from engaging in pursuit.

They dashed off, leaving the vendor yelling and screaming. The boy I was going to speak to, looked directly at me, then rushed off with the group, obviously a member of this gang of thieves. They raced up the middle of the camp, around the corner of another stall, and into the cover of the wagons.

I decided to follow the bandits. After all, they were still kids, and I needed to talk to them. I hoped they could help, maybe my last resort. I made my way through the maze of wagons and found the boys laughing and patting each other on the back. Then they sensed my presence, and I was suddenly the object of several ugly stares.

I just stared back. They looked at each other as I started to advance. They panicked, dropped the sack, separated, and scurried off between the wagons. I walked over and picked up the scattered fruit, placing all items back into the sack. I held one large peach in my hand and brought it closer to my face. I could smell the sweetness. The aroma was intoxicating, especially for someone who had not really eaten for what seemed like weeks.

The temptation was overwhelming; I had to take a bite. I opened my mouth and closed my eyes. This was going to be heaven. Then I stopped. For some unknown reason, I just couldn't do it. I could not eat this luscious piece of fruit. I had food and refreshment right in my hands, at my fingertips, but I still had no assistance and no direction as to which way to go. Eating this fruit was not going to get me any closer to home. There were probably many roads out of this encampment, and I needed to know which one to take. What to do now?

I leaned against the wagon, drooling at the sight of the mouthwatering peach, I could taste it, but I could not eat it. Like the tale of Adam and Eve and the forbidden fruit. The story was a little different than mine as I remember, but the outcome wasn't very good. Adam must have been too hungry or really stupid, I can't recall. Anyways, they got the boot from the Garden of Eden and ended up in hell, I guess. I was in hell now and had to find my way out. I wasn't about to make things worse by satisfying my hunger and thirst with this golden orb. After all, this fruit was not mine to eat. Yes I found it, but I know how it got here.

I did not pay for the fruit or receive it with permission. Not withstanding the receipt of any assistance in my quest, or reward, I must return the fruit to the vendor, all of it, every single piece. This was an easy decision because the fruit was not mine. Case closed, nothing more to think about. I placed the peach inside the bag and headed back to the fruit stand lumbering down the main thoroughfare, bag in hand.

No one even looked at me. When I arrived, the vendor was in the process of organizing his stall which had been vandalized by the band of thieves.

He looked up from behind the boxes and noticed me

standing there. He stopped, folded his arms, and stared at me, as if to ask, what do you want? I held out the bag and sat it on the stand. He opened the sack and peered inside. Not much expression, no nod of thanks, he just looked at me, than looked inside the bag once again. Maybe he was taking inventory, making sure all the missing fruit was there. I guessed I had done my duty, so it was time to leave and see if I could find help, certainly none was coming from here. I had to convince someone, to at least show me the correct direction out of this makeshift village.

Hands in my pockets, I again made my way up the hard-pan runway. Soon after my departure, I felt a strong hand on my shoulder. I stopped and turned. The vendor was behind me. He moved along to my side and began to guide me up the street. We passed the many stalls and turned into an area where the majority of the wagons were parked. He led me to a large ornately decorated wagon with three stairs leading through a curtain-like doorway. He entered but I stayed behind. I guess he expected me to follow, but I felt slightly uninvited and uncomfortable. A few seconds later, a pleasant, attractive looking woman poked her head around the curtain and signaled for me to enter. Seeing the woman helped me relax, a mother son thing I guess, so I skipped up the stairs and stepped inside.

The interior was interesting to say the least. Cluttered with knickknacks and colourful banners adorning the walls, the cramped quarters seemed cozy and homey. I was offered a seat, so obliged. The woman disappeared behind a second curtain while the vendor sat opposite me. The woman appeared with bread, fried chicken, and freshly cooked vegetables. A feast for a king I thought. My gastric juices began to unwind and I couldn't wait to dig in. The couple spoke in some unfamiliar language, nothing I could interpret.

Then they gave me the go sign. I wanted to devour the meal like a ravaged animal, but controlled myself, finding my manners.

The woman poured me a large glass of cold milk and I began to eat, savouring every morsel. The food was delicious, not because I was famished, the food was really delicious. I tried not to show my enthusiasm for the meal, but I got the impression they knew I was starving. Hunger is hard to hide.

The couple finished long before I did. They sat and watched my polite, yet voracious attack upon their banquet, I was famished. Eyes all over me, the couple remained without much expression, not a smile or a sound. I stopped and could take no more. My belly full, I knew it was time to give in. My eyes had been bigger than my stomach, but I finished everything on my plate. I sat back rubbing my stomach. I absolutely could not move. That was great. The woman started clearing the table while the vendor picked his teeth and staring off into space.

There was no where else to go in this smallish enclosure, the table being the focal point of the room. I am sure my bedroom is larger. This was kind of like living in an overgrown camper. I once again scanned the living area, trying to anticipate what would happen next. I was hoping I could somehow convince them to assist me, but I could not speak their language. I was starting to worry. Maybe this would be my only chance at help, but end up with none. The vendor kept an eye on me, maybe suspicious of anyone in his home. Hope he didn't think I would try to steal anything. He couldn't be thinking that, I had just returned his fruit? People are funny. You never know what is going through someone's mind.

The woman came out from behind the curtain carrying something covered with a silk cloth. She set it on the table and removed the royal blue shroud, revealing

a crystal ball, a real one, like from the movies, how cool. This woman must be a psychic, or fortune teller. I guess she was going to show me how it works. I felt very privileged to receive a private audience with the village clairvoyant. She placed a lighted candle on the table and stared at my face, then into my eyes. I have to admit I started to feel a little awkward being the centre of her attention. If I didn't know better, I had to think she was reading my face, all the lines, curvatures, features. Not sure what she was hoping to accomplish, maybe just part of her routine.

A minute or so passed, the study session over, she turned her focus to the mystical orb. I was unsure of what I was about to witness, but whatever it was, she was dead serious about her business. No doubt about that. Scary serious!

She maneuvered her hands over top the sphere, chanting words I could not distinguish. An opaque cloud formed inside the ball, undulating round and round. I honestly saw nothing unusual, but her facial expressions told a different story. The woman became very animated and emotional. Her hands waving frantically in the air, she began to mutter and murmur, maybe some kind of incantation or mystical chant. Not sure, but really quite frightening. After several minutes, her hands stopped, her eyes bulged, and she jumped up quickly covering her precious globe. I was surprised at the reaction, not a good omen I suspect, and looked at the vendor who was looking at the woman. She muttered and whispered something once again, causing even the vendor to look perplexed. Cradled like a babe in arms, she removed the ball back behind the curtain from whence it came. She never returned. I never heard a sound from behind the heavy drape, no indication as to what she had seen. I guess the show was over.

The vendor stood. I took this as my signal to leave. The vendor retrieved a sack from the counter and placed some fruit, bread, and a small container of water inside. He handed it to me and directed me to follow him outside. The vendor led the way out of the maze of trailers and into an open pasture outside the village proper. I followed him. There were many roads leading out of the village, so I was lucky to have him as my guide. Now four hundred or so metres from the village, the vendor stopped and pointed to a trail leading once again into a sparsely treed forest. He gave me one last look and then headed back toward the encampment.

The vendor had never muttered so much as a sound to me the whole time. Strange, but he was good enough to show me the way. I guess this was it, the path I must follow. My belly full, batteries recharged, I still had enough light to guide me into the forest.

I turned to take one last look at the village, wondering what the woman had seen in the crystal ball. That part was creepy weird. I wondered what she had murmured to the vendor.

What a bizarre reaction? I will never forget it. As I turned, the wind whipped up and began howling through the trees. A wall of heat rippled the air in front of me, obscuring my vision and causing my eyes blink rapidly. I covered my face and then felt coolness. I looked up and the village was gone, vanished into thin air, not a ghost in sight.

Astonishing I thought. What is happening? Where did everything and everyone go? Impossible...was I really there? I must have been because I had a sack full of food. Wow...what is going on and why am I in the middle of it? I had been doing a lot of head shaking lately with no indication it would end any time soon. I glanced skyward for a solution, but the clear blue ceiling offered none. I became mesmerized by the passing clouds as my mind revisited a different time.

I remembered walking to the bus stop one Saturday morning, going about a kilometre across town to visit my friend. I was too lazy to walk, so I thought I would take the bus. The pedestrian traffic was light that morning. I strolled down the sidewalk noticing only one person, a young girl, about fifty metres ahead of me. I noticed something fall from her wallet as she jostled with the awkwardness of her large handbag. I could only guess she was rushing to organize the contents as she looked back, sighting the arrival of the bus. I believed the object was merely a piece of paper. She reached the bus stop and waited, the bus approaching. I began jogging to ensure I could catch the same bus. I slowed to look at the paper that had fallen from the girl's wallet, a twenty dollar bill. The bus stopped and the doors opened. I picked up the money and could have rushed up to the bus and boarded, but I hesitated and decided not to. I watched the doors close and the bus depart. I had twenty dollars more than I had yesterday, a good start to my day indeed. I always said, "finder's keepers...loser's weepers."No one would return the money if I had lost it. Her loss is my gain, that's just the way it goes. I put the money in my pocket and felt this was my lucky day.

I also recalled the time I took some apples from old man Wilson's apple tree. He was a mean old guy and everyone knew he hated kids. He lived at the end of the block, in a large, poorly kept, wood frame, two story house. He never came outside, just screamed at anyone who tried to take the apples off his tree.

The apple tree was ancient, but the apples were delicious. Every season, the neighbourhood kids and even many adults would help themselves to the fruit dangling near the fence line. One of the branches even hung outside the property, and the apples were easy pickings.

Everyone did it, so why shouldn't I. Reaching over the fence to snare an apple or two was a little risky because he always seemed to be watching. I guess he had nothing else to do, except scare little kids. I think this was our revenge. I would sometimes reach over the fence and pull the branch outside the property, snatch an apple and then run like crazy. Sometimes I was lucky and never got caught even though I always felt he was watching. The branch hanging over the fence, outside the property, I thought was fair game, and didn't really belong to him.

The funny thing is, even though everyone thought Mr. Wilson hated kids, we never heard anything from our parents. I mean, Mr. Wilson never told on us even though he knew us all very well. He could have reported us, but never did. Maybe if I had just asked him for an apple, he would have given one to me. Or maybe if I had offered to help him picked the apples, he would have given me some. Never thought of it at the time, it always seemed easier just to take them. I had no problem with that, never lost any sleep over it, never got into trouble for doing it, so why not?

The clouds eclipsed the sun, causing me to blink my eyes, and stop day dreaming. Back to the business at hand. I had to get back home. My family must be worried.

I headed towards the beckoning trail, spotting my little friend, the blue jay, perched atop a small tree. I smiled and waved. It spread its wings in reply and flew off into the distance. Then I heard it again. I now knew the tell tale signs, but never knew quite what to expect. The Voice was returning, so I halted and impatiently listened.

"RECTITUDE is moral virtue or strength. Rectitude is the power of deciding upon a certain course of conduct in accordance with reason and what is right and what is wrong. This done without wavering. It is a consequence of being honest and honourable."

"Rectitude is simply, the ability to make the right decision, respecting all equally, seeking justice, doing the right thing. This type of character is not borne of mere intellectual understanding. It is much more an instinctive and intuitive understanding of that which is naturally good and just. The righteous man walks with integrity."

The Voice faded and was gone. Again no help! Only mumbo jumbo. How was I supposed to make any sense out of this? How is this helping me get back home? I was frustrated and becoming more confused as to when all this would end. What was next? I was starting to boil over, so closed my eyes and kept telling myself, this will all end soon, very soon. Eyes open, I adjusted my focus. I had no option but to press onward, time to move.

FIVE

The River

THE PATH WIDENED IN THIS PART OF THE FOREST, light sufficient to bless my advance. I still had to be observant because I had no idea what part of the world I was in, only contemplating an educated guess. I could be just about anywhere. My journey through the thinly treed acreage was tedious and boring. I had gotten used to the sounds, so should be automatically alerted to any telltale noise that did not fit in. My walking stick was a useful crutch, not to help me walk, but as a support weapon in the event of danger. I kind of felt like Robin Hood in Sherwood Forest. Only I did not have a band of merry men.

Must have been late afternoon when the trees finally parted and I could see a large clearing up ahead. I emerged from the delicate canopy into the brilliant sunlight. I used my arms to shade my eyes, and then I heard it...water. Lowering my arm slowly, I was almost afraid to look. Directly in front of me, not more than a hundred metres away, was a river. Not the same river from the vanishing canyon. This one was wide, the current slow and powerful. The water was murky and possibly very deep. Not sure if this was the Nile, Amazon, or the mighty Mississippi. I panned the area looking for a bridge, but there was none. I made my way to the riverbank and looked carefully up and down either side. There appeared to be no path or way around to the opposite side.

I was a good swimmer, but this challenge would be much too difficult. A river like this, at least three hundred metres wide, could have a massive under current or whirlpools that could drag me beneath the

43

surface in a second. Swimming across would be much too dangerous. Unfortunately, the path lead here and from what I could see, continued on the other side.

What was I going to do now? Maybe I could build a raft or a boat? How, I had nothing useful at my disposal? Staring into the muddy waterway, I started to think of the things I could not see. What really lived in this river? What lie below the sediment laden surface? I imagined giant crocodiles, monolithic serpents, river sharks, and flesh eating piranhas. Anything or all were possible. Nothing would surprise me. There could even be something down there worse than all of these. My imagination was running wild, and not in a good way.

I wandered around the clearing looking for materials, anything that might assist my crossing. Situation hopeless...this was not a hardware store. There were many fallen trees, but no way to bind them together safely. I looked for some divine inspiration, but received none. I guess I had to do this the hard way, figure it out by myself. I looked for an hour or so, and came up empty. I thought it best to have a seat and formulate a strategy. One that wouldn't get me killed. Nothing came to mind, and I was growing impatient. I picked up some stones and began targeting the trees on the other side of the clearing. With thick trunks and not too far away, I could finally vent some of my frustration. I was the Aurora Little League's best pitcher, so I would have a little fun seeing how many I could hit. After many hits and misses, I remained vexed and perturbed. I walked over to the bank of trees, picked up a large rock, and hurled it as hard as I could.

CRACK! A direct hit, bulls-eye.

My uncanny accuracy caused such a vibration, that a large chunk of tree barked came loose and fell to the ground. At first, I shrugged it off as a dead soldier, than the light bulb came on. This could be interesting? A fortuitous strike by chance. I examined the section of concave bark measuring about two inches thick, and approximately four feet in length. The slice of tree skin looked like a dugout canoe. One end was curled, providing partial closure for the opening.

I thought I could wedge some branches and leaves width ways across, sealing up both ends. Might work, should float, but would it stay together. This appeared to be the closest thing to a boat I would find out here.

Quite by accident, I may have found my salvation. I gathered some branches to fix up the open ends and then searched for a pair of oars. With sticks and branches everywhere, suitable oars were easy to locate. I prepared the canoe with meticulous detail and then stared at my handiwork. Good job I thought. It better be...better float. My life depended on it. A regular Thor Heyerdahl, sailing across the Pacific aboard his hand made raft. I think he survived, can't remember, I hope so, yeah I think he did.

Time to eat some of the vendor's fresh fruit and bread, assess the risk, bolster my confidence, then I should be good to go. I took the fruit from the sack, was about to indulge, but was rudely interrupted by a sound, a voice, but not *"the"* *Voice*. I looked around and saw nothing. I was about to take my first bite, when I heard it again. I was almost afraid to look, if fact, I didn't look, I just ignored it. Then I felt it. I sensed another presence, like someone watching me, staring at me. I slowly lifted my head and turned.

Holy macaroni! Can cows fly? I bobbled my peach, snatching it before the fruit kissed the ground. Not a hundred metres away, a frail, old woman stood motionless near the middle of the clearing. Straggly gray hair covering half her face, she was dressed in shabby clothes, looked like an unmade bed, quite a mess. Her face was pale, wrinkled, and she looked extremely weak. She said nothing, just stood there. Where did she come from? How did she get here? I had hoped help was on the way, but this was no cavalry, and someone with one foot in the grave could not possibly be of any assistance. Now what? I hope she can speak, English would be good.

I noticed her looking at the fruit in my hand, so I knew she was hungry. I extended my hand, offering her the peach. The old woman stepped cautiously forward and she took it readily, taking baby bites and chewing unhurriedly. I offered her a seat on a log, so she sat and ate. We both finished our lunch in silence and then she spoke in a very faint voice. She needed to rejoin her family and must get across the river.

If I assisted her to cross, she said she new the way I needed to go, and would help me. Not sure how she knew where I needed to go, but an interesting proposition, in an event. Big problem, red flag, you guessed it. The canoe had only room for one, and now there were two. What was I going to do now?

My brilliant strategy could now be thrown right out the window. Back to the drawing board! It was blatantly obvious the old woman could not swim, and was too weak to do much of anything. I never once thought of leaving her behind, but became increasingly worried about our situation.

We both had to cross the river. What was the best solution? I guess there was only one. I had to place her inside the canoe. Possibly she could use the oars to help keep the canoe on line? I would have to swim along side, thread water, and try to propel the canoe forward from the back and side. This was not going to be easy. The distance we had to travel was not insignificant. I could only hope the river would cooperate a little, wishful thinking I know. I related the plan to the old woman and she looked calmly out into the river.

Okay...I guess ignoring me means we should give it a shot.

I dragged the vessel to the bank and set it in the water. The old woman followed. Wading out to my knees, I helped the old woman board the canoe. She sat down and held the oars ready to place them in the water. When I thought she was balanced and prepared to row, I started my part of the job.

I pushed the canoe out further until my feet could no longer touch bottom. I held on to the left side with my left hand and the back with my right hand. I started to propel the boat forward using me leg power. The old woman began to row as best she could. We moved slowly but steadily in a fairly straight line. This just might work I thought to myself, it better work.

No telling how deep the water beneath me, but from time to time I could feel the undertow push against my legs. I hoped that's what it was? The river was littered with debris. Tree branches, pieces of sod, logs and pieces of wood drifted past, some of it bouncing off our hull and me. I just prayed a large log would not capsize our miniature titanic. We were at the mercy of the river.

I tried to look from side to side and keep a straight course. I was constantly spitting out foul tasting water and shaking my head to remove it from my face. I had to keep my vision clear. I had to be able to see everything around me.

The current took us down the river slightly, but not too far. The water continuously splashed my face and sometimes got into my eyes, blinding me momentarily. I noticed several large objects bobbing up and down in the water. Just wood and logs I presumed. Suddenly, a splash to my left drew my attention. I could not catch sight of it, but assumed a fish had come out looking for food. From time to time the canoe would sway with the current and I would struggle to correct the line. The old woman was getting weary and I told her to rest. I kept on pushing, she just steered.

On the far bank I observed a huge animal, larger than a horse, some kind of humongous deer, maybe an elk. The antlers spanning at least two metres, this majestic creature had come to the riverbank for a drink. Lowering its head into the water for a few seconds then jumping back quickly, the jittery elk repeated this series of motions several times. Fascinating...but why so nervous? Reflexes on auto pilot I guess. Now refreshed, it decided to wade into the river and start swimming across. Wild animals were excellent swimmers, a built in survival and security feature. I watched its progress, seemed to have a good little motor. I looked at the old woman who started to row methodically once again and at the same time heard a loud splash. I thought it might be a beaver slapping its tail on the water as a signal, but my guess was wrong. Turning in the direction of the splash, I could not locate any other animals, or the elk. The huge creature was gone, vanished beneath the surface with no signs of resurfacing, how odd?

Unlikely an animal of that size would just disappear from sight so quickly. Maybe the under current dragged it down, or it got caught in a violent whirlpool. I had no time to ponder its demise. I had to worry about my own demise...or our own.

We were about halfway now and I was getting fatigued. The old woman kept rowing as we nibbled away at the intended distance. Suddenly, the old woman stopped and I looked up at her. She was looking at the river.

I followed her line of sight, but could not really see anything from my vantage point. She seemed different, scared, frozen...paralyzed. I looked again, scanning the surface, noticing something floating in our direction.

I did not like the look of this. I was hoping just an

errant log, but I saw what I didn't want to see. A monster of a crocodile was eying us with particular interest. I could see the black eyes, nostrils, the hunched back and the tip of the tale forming a wake as it advanced. The beast had to be twenty feet long. The elk's disappearance was no longer a mystery. The river could be full of these creatures. Maybe what I had felt before was no current, but the crocodiles checking out the prey. This enormous predator has a voracious appetite, the ultimate eating machine. We had to get to the other side now, but I didn't know how. I could only swim so fast and the old woman was traumatized. With the old woman in this condition, my job became much more difficult. I needed to muster some speed from somewhere, but could not. I was tired and scared. I swam as fast as I could, but the crocodile glided through the water with ease. We would be no match for this mighty beast.

The croc submerged, signaling its intention to attack. This torpedo of death was no doubt making an underwater beeline for us, an easy meal on its mind I would imagine. I had to get out of the water and into the canoe while I still had my legs. I hoisted myself into the craft which was now taking on water. How many more things could go wrong? My handiwork was beginning to spawn leak after leak. More debris kept bumping into us and piling up along side. I sensed the croc wasn't far away either. The tension was unbearable, this waiting game terrifying. I grabbed my walking stick to use as a weapon, hoping I could poke out one of its eyes and scare the underwater assassin away.

I saw the creature penetrate the surface about a metre away. This was the moment of truth, or death. No time for fear, I must fight for our lives with my last breath. I poised my staff, holding on with both hands, and then it came. Out of the water, jaws agape. At that exact instant, a gigantic piece of sod smashed into our canoe. Instinctively I grabbed the old woman and catapulted the two of us out of the canoe and onto the miniature floating island.

The crocodile's jaws clamped down on the small dugout, crushing the entire structure. The gnashing of teeth then an explosion of sawdust was all I saw and heard from my vantage point. The croc disappeared beneath the surface again. A mouth full of wood...definitely not on the menu. This croc is going to be choked. The meal that got away! Maybe not yet, we were still very vulnerable.

The piece of earth we landed on was about two metres in diameter and floated along with the current. A small tree situated in the middle of the island provided us something to hang onto. I could not believe our good fortune. I looked to the heavens and said a thank you. The old woman was stunned and shaken. I only hoped I had not harmed her when I yanked her wildly out of the canoe. I guess we were safe for now, no croc in sight, just had to figure out how to get to the other side. Maybe the current would take us there, just a little farther down stream. I let out a sigh of relief.

The woman pointed over my shoulder. I looked at her face. I was perplexed. She should feel safe. I turned to see the water coming to an end. I could now hear the water cascading over the edge...a waterfall dead ahead. My staff was useless in trying to steer the massive piece of sod. We were only about fifty metres from shore, too close to die now.

I used my staff to try and locate the bottom, I could not. This area of the river was still very deep and the croc or crocs were still down there. Getting back in the water may be a bad idea. I could not risk the old woman's life, there must be another way.

50

I racked my brain for a quick answer, but my attention was again taken away by the old woman tapping me on the shoulder. I had a bad feeling my worst fears were about to be realized...yes our old friend was back.

I turned to see the croc's huge snout break the surface and propel towards us, on the attack again. A man eating beast or a deadly waterfall! What a choice...of how to die. Neither was appealing, but there seemed no miracle in sight...or was there? To my left, I noticed more action in the river. An unusual swirl in the water indicated something was moving towards the crocodile. The monster was within a few metres when suddenly a gigantic serpent made its move on the unsuspecting crocodile.

I had never seen a snake of this scale. Anaconda, python, boa, who knows, but it wrapped itself around the croc, which immediately went into a death roll. Thrashing and writhing in the waters, one trying to subdue the other. A monumental battle was underway. The croc took them both beneath the surface. I focused on the waterfall thinking the two predators would keep each other busy for a long time, I hoped. The waterfall was now only a hundred metres away and we were both terrified. Then I felt something unusual.

For some reason, the patch of floating grass seemed to be getting closer to the riverbank, yet we did nothing to assist it. Closer and closer, the entire piece of sod began to rise out of the water. Now elevated above the surface, we stared at each other, amazed and confused. What was happening? I reacted in desperation, expecting the worst. I looked into the water and saw huge flippers and then a huge green scaly head. My heart pounded furiously for several seconds, then began to settle.

Underneath us was a giant tortoise, river turtle,

whatever you want to call it. This incredible creature was about to save our lives. Our little piece of paradise was actually attached to the back of this abnormally large amphibian. The tortoise swam for the riverbank, having no intention of going over the falls. We held onto the tree and steadied ourselves for the ride.

Only a few metres to go! Suddenly...the unthinkable happened. The croc was back and coming with the speed of a nuclear warhead. The ferocious reptile had revenge on its mind and took dead aim at us. Like a bullet train, closer and closer. Jaws unhinged, and closing in fast, I took the old woman and leaped the final metre to the safety of the soggy bank. The Goliath creature clamped down on the tortoise and dragged it back into the depths of the river. We scrambled to safety, our hearts thumping like drummers gone crazy. I was certain the entire forest could hear them beating. Our unfortunate savior had met an untimely end, but I was sure it would enter super turtle heaven for his sacrificial good deed.

We were terrified, wet, and overwhelmed, but still in one piece, alive. I looked at the old woman and saw tears stream down her cheek. Not sure if those were tears of happiness, joy, or fright. Either way, we had survived. Since crocodiles also live on land I thought it best we get out of the area right away.

The path was visibly evident, so I helped the old woman to her feet and guided her out of the danger zone. We must have walked for a half mile or so, than feeling much safer, I knew we both had to rest. My fruit, bread, and water were gone, nothing left, or so I thought. However, the old woman surprised me when she pulled two apples and the little water container from a huge pocket on her dress. Boy... was I glad to see that. I smiled and we ate and drank what she had salvaged. Hopefully we would be able to locate some food and drink tomorrow. We would camp here for the night, seemed safe enough. I looked for a suitable place to settle down, than heard a chirp. I followed the sound to the top of a rotted tree stump where the blue jay stood, bobbing its majestic crown from side to side. The ability to fly must be great I thought, sure could have used that today. I was really exhausted and I am sure the old woman was as well, time to sleep.

I sat on the soft bed of grass, closed my eyes, and began to recall the time I witnessed an old man and old woman on an escalator. I was sure they were in their eighties, skinny and weak looking. I was about eight steps behind them as they reached the bottom.

The old man could not lift his foot in a timely manner and was knocked off balance by the kick-plate on the floor. The old woman struggled to keep him upright. The old man tried to grasp the moving rail with his right hand and balance himself using his cane in the other. The escalator kept moving and the two seniors had to fight with all their might not to fall backwards against the sharp metal stairs.

I could have rushed down to assist but did nothing, what's the point, they'll be okay. They barely escaped disaster as I reached the bottom and passed by. Finally off the escalator, they were huffing and puffing, exhausted and scared. They should watch what they are doing, be more careful, I thought. Old people should know better.

On another occasion, I decided to take the outside stairs down from the flight over instead of taking the escalator inside the mall. I was in a hurry to meet my friend and was already late, this detour would save time. Halfway down, I encountered an old woman holding onto the railing with one hand and using her cane to help negotiate the stairwell.

All I could think of was...why is she here? She

should be in the mall on the escalator, what an old fool. She was blocking the entire stairwell, and I couldn't get by. I hummed and cleared my throat, but she didn't budge. I thought she must be old and deaf too. Why now, I am in a hurry, get out of my way.

I jockeyed from right to left, making it obvious, I was trying to get by. Finally, I could not wait any longer. Impatience got the best of me. I pushed my way around her and scurried down the stairs. I was so annoyed, especially when my friend scolded me for being late. Stupid old woman I thought. At the time, I could not envision myself ever being in the same state. I was very impolite, impatient, and inconsiderate. I should have helped her, not ignored her struggle. I found it impossible for me to realize, one day I will be old as well. I never thought about that day ever coming, but I guess it will. In a similar position, I would hope someone would offer assistance. Guess I'll just have to wait and see.

I opened my eyes and laid my head on a small log. I was just about to doze off. My eyes popped open as I thought the old woman was trying talk to me, maybe something was wrong. Alas, the sound was not coming from her, it was the Voice.

"BENEVOLENCE characterizes the true goodness of the mind, unbiased kindness and altruism. I converts thought and regard for the welfare of other people, and finds expression in sympathy, gentleness, compassion, and charitableness."

"BENEVOLENCE is a feeling of good towards all, founded on the understanding that we are all essentially the same and should be treated as such. This virtue requires life long practice and discipline beginning with empathy for others in distress.

The Voice dissipated once again, leaving its message for me to contemplate. Like I had time? I had been to busy tying to stay alive, and then had to listen to the Voice. The only thing I want to hear from the voice is, "This is over...tomorrow you are going home." That is all I want to hear, nothing else thank you. We'll see.

I glanced over at the old woman who appeared to be fast asleep. Not sure if I could sleep. If not, I guess I could count crocodiles.

SIX

The Tree

I WAS UP WITH THE BIRDS, but noticed the old woman had preceded me. It didn't take long to spot her. She was scouting the tree line for something, food I guess, that's what I hoped anyway. Maybe she knew where to look, because I sure didn't, not my kind of grocery store. I was hungry, we both were, but not much to find there I would suspect. She returned with a few berries, a bit of a surprise, and shared them with me. Quite tasty considering...and a nice gesture on her part. I had a few walnuts left, so we finished those as well. The two of us wandered over to some broad leaf ferns and licked off the morning dew. What a breakfast, fantastic...just joking of course, I was getting used to this, not a good thing.

The old woman seemed to be nice enough, and I know she was doing the best she could. My main concern now was our progress. Would the old woman slow me down? I prayed she really new the way and we could recommend some short cuts? In that case, it's possible she could save us time, and I could return home faster. I had no idea why I was worried about time, I had nothing but time.

Starving to death should be my main concern. Not much food available out in the middle of nowhere, or maybe I really just didn't know where to look, or what to look for. At home, my much maligned survival skills incorporated such drastic measures as a short walk to the refrigerator. My other major concern...my now greater responsibility. I was now taking care of two instead of just myself, which was difficult enough. A lot of pressure for any one person, let alone a kid. I could not fathom the outcome. I didn't want to. I might as well put my quick return home on the shelf for the time being because there was nothing quick about the old woman. The only thing I could think of was the hare and tortoise syndrome. Slow and steady prevails, quick and reckless fails. Now I'm depending on Aesop and his fabulous fables. I am really in trouble.

I could only try to keep it together because now we both had to survive and be prepared for whatever was around the next corner. Her knowing the way was a big plus, should be the advantage I need, the game saver. I sure hoped she did know the way, my life depended on it.

We started off, and shortly into our trek, the path seemed to fizzle out and was no more. Now I really had to rely on her local knowledge. She trudged along, leading the way, like a bloodhound in pursuit. After all, she should know her way home. We marched over undulating terrain and rolling hills, until coming upon another lightly forested area. Without hesitation the old woman forged ahead. I followed, surprised at her stamina. Another hour or so and I noticed we had been climbing.   Even though the incline had been very subtle, we were now at a noticeable elevation.

The old woman stopped for a breather on top of a knoll. Being close behind, I stopped and viewed the area. To our left was the side of a large hill, maybe 50 metres high, but my vision was limited as to what was around the bend. There was a narrow path leading up the side of the hill, fairly steep, a challenge for the old woman. To the right, another narrow trail leading down the hill into a tiny valley of sorts. I looked at the old woman and she seemed indecisive as to which way to go. I had butterflies in my stomach waiting for her to make the choice, the high road or the low road. Hand to her chin, she pondered the two possibilities.

Her having to make such a determined evaluation about a direction she should be familiar with, was making me nervous and anxious. Guessing was not a good strategy...we had to know for sure. I had to step in and say something, my life was at stake.

Since I could clearly see the valley from the top of the upper path, I suggested we split up. I would travel the upper path because the climb would be too strenuous for her, and the old woman would travel the lower path into the valley. I could keep an eye on her from above, so I presumed that we would both be safe. This way we could see which path would eventually join up with the original trail, or so I thought. She nodded and slowly started her decent. I began my climb keeping a close watch. I gave the old woman my walking stick to assist with her descent down the slope.

As I lumbered up the grassy path, I noticed the footpath becoming increasingly narrower and narrower. Soon I was actually rubbing against the hillside. I saw the old woman far below about to reach the valley floor. I estimated I was about one hundred metres above her at this point. I don't like heights, but had to glance down on occasion to check on the old woman.

I proceeded, hoping my course of action would provide an answer as to which route was correct. I didn't want it to be this one. If so, the old woman would have to come back up here, or I would have to go and get her and bring her back. That would be a huge effort and waist of time. First things first, I wanted to see where this hillside byway would take me. I kept on cautiously, hoping the grassy path would widen, but the walkway soon became more of a ledge. This was not good.

My footing was becoming precarious and I was feeling a increasingly unsure of my decision to follow this daredevil's tightrope. The dry grass was actually quite slippery and there was not much room to maneuver. I glanced once again at the old woman far below. She was making headway down in the valley, not concerned for me in the least. That was okay, I just hoped she would locate the trail we needed, the one she was supposed to know, the one that better be there. I kept advancing, but was starting to slip and slide more and more. I pressed myself against the hillside for support. This path is going to disappear soon and I could be stranded here. I was beginning to sweat bullets contemplating what mishap may be in store just around the next corner.

For a moment, I lost sight of the old woman and leaned forward to see if I could spot her from above. I took a bad step and hit a patch of shiny long brown grass. My leg gave way and I was down on one knee, my balance compromised. I began to slide forward, then sideways.

I tried grabbing handfuls of grass, but my weight shifted and I was slowly going down. Feet first, I desperately tried to dig in my heels, but could not penetrate the thick layers of grass. I was beginning to pick up speed and the terrifying thought of a long tumble down this grassy bank was not for faint of heart, not mine for sure. Right now I was not in the mood for a roller coaster ride down a hundred metre cliff. Give me a break...please stop!

Within seconds, I had lost complete control, at the mercy of the slippery slope. I had given my walking stick to the old woman, so had no added assistance. The stick would have been of little use. Now I had to rely on my athletic abilities to cope with the situation. There was no way I could keep track of the old woman now while trying desperately to survive the plunge. Turning in circles, I noticed a ridge a few metres ahead...disaster. How was I going to escape this calamity? Appearing there be no way out this time, I hit the furrow and became airborne. I was dead for sure, that was all I could think of while sailing through the air. I was destined to land on some jagged rocks or be slammed against the bottom of the valley. Either way the outcome would be catastrophic, possibly fatal, or worse, pancake city.

The feeling of falling down an open elevator shaft lasted only seconds as I quickly came face to face with the canopy of a gigantic tree. I crashed through the primary layer of branches, escorted gently downward atop the multi-tiered mantle, which had kindly broken my fall instead of my neck.

Not exactly like falling on a haystack, but I guess this was a close second. My impromptu tumble came to a sudden halt. I was sure I had been branded with many scratches and scrapes, now stranded high above the ground, in a tree top of all places. Face down, I had a clear view of the ground below and was afraid to move. I didn't want to fall now, I would really get hurt. I was a long way up. I grabbed onto the branches for support and weaved my way carefully downwards to the top of the trunk.

This burly tree must have been as thick as a house. I could not really see forward through the dense leafy branches, but could see the ground. Wow...must be ten stories high...Yikes. I hate heights, but I was now closer to the ground now than I was a few seconds ago.

I looked around for the old woman, but could not locate her, and was worried. Where was she? How could I get down from here? I had to find her? Maybe she had found the way and left me for lost? Gone without me...great?

What a quandary. I looked around, and a few feet away to my right, I noted a hole in the trunk, a large hole. I shuffled over to a better vantage point and peered into the hole. I was shocked. The massive tree trunk seemed to have been hollowed out. It was incredible. It looked like there was a built in ladder leading down into the cavity of the massive tree trunk. So curious, I thought. I balanced myself, turned accordingly, and began my decent down the ladder, into belly of the whale. I felt like Alice in Wonderland falling into the rabbit hole...kind of cool.

Once inside, I observed the interior and all its comforts, such as a seat, a ledge, and a bench that could be used for a bed. Surely not a natural formation, but maybe, really no indication the unique outgrowths were manufactured. The inside resembled an imaginatively contrived tree-house. This was really amazing. I could live here. Wish I could show my friends this. What a great place to hang out, escape from the drudgery of the real world, and relax unopposed. Home sweet home. Just the sight of all this brought a smile to my face, not many of those lately.

There was even a hole on one side to serve as a window. I stuck my head through and looked down. Wow...amazing...great view! Back inside I marveled at the find and then something peculiar caught my attention. On the bench-like formation, I saw the outline of what looked like a map, possibly a map of the area, possibly a map that could assist me in returning home faster. I certainly hoped so. On closer study, I saw chalk markings of what could possibly be a river, mountain, village, and an arrow showing the way. I started to bubble with excitement. How fortunate I thought. Someone must know the area and had detailed the bench with their handiwork. The markings were definitely not fresh, here for some time I'd guess. Nevertheless, I was ecstatic with the discovery.

The tree had saved my life and now was hopefully

going to show me the way home. I was confident this was the case. The map was quite detailed and would need some intense study to memorize. I gave the map my undivided attention until I remembered the old woman. Oh man...I better look for her, she could be in trouble.

I rushed to peek out the porthole, my eyes searching in all directions. Finally, there she was, far below. I was high above, inside a tree. No way would she be able to find me here. I waited until she passed directly below and then I shouted. She looked around, confused as to where my voice was coming from. I instructed her to look up. I stuck my hand out the hole and waved frantically, then my head...big smile. She looked upward and gave me an awful stare, like what the heck was I doing up there?

I looked around and saw what looked like the outline of a doorway. Couldn't be...could it? I stuck my finger nails into a small space and pulled. It was a door, a bark door, which opened onto a platform. I stepped outside and there I found a pulley complete with ropes and a pallet that could be lowered to the ground. I guess this was the elevator. I untangled the ropes and started to lower the scaffold. When the small podium arrived at ground level, I motioned for the old woman to climb aboard and hang on. She hesitated, then cautiously stepped onto the pallet and held onto the rope.

I grabbed the rope and began to pull. The mechanism was well designed because raising the tiny stage was quite effortless. I pulled slowly and steadily as not to cause the scaffolding to shift. After a few minutes of not so strenuous labour, the old woman had arrived on the top tier. She looked at me as if to say, how did you find this place, and how did you get here? I smiled and shrugged. What could I say, a miracle. She took an inquisitive look around and we moved inside.

Stepping around the small confines gingerly, she eyeballed the interior. I was sure she was as surprised as me. I thought it a good idea for her to stay and rest while. I would lower myself to the valley floor and look for food. She agreed, so in my excitement, I quickly stepped back onto the outdoor podium, grabbed the ropes, and made my departure.

Once on the ground, I could see the full extent of this immense tree. What a tree...phenomenal! I began my search and luckily found some berries. I thought I would spend some extra time looking for something I could use for a pen and paper. I wanted to copy the map so I could take it with me. Not a stationery store in sight, the forest refused to provide me with the necessary supplies. I knew this was too much to ask, but I had to try.

Along the tree line I found some birch bark and a sharp stone. I tested the bark and the stone did leave some marks, so thought it possible I may be able to replicate the map onto the birch bark using my rock pen.

Proud of my food and paper-pen findings, I hustled back to the dumbwaiter. I hoisted myself back to the top of the majestic timber and stepped inside. The old woman was lying on the bench, fast asleep. I never thought anything about it, just took a seat, placing the berries, birch bark, and rock pen, on another small ledge. I thought the old woman would be happy to see the food, so it was my turn to catch a few winks.

I guess I must have dozed off for an hour or so, waking to see the old woman looking out the porthole. I stretched, yawned, and stood up, drawing her attention. I showed her the berries which I am sure she had already seen. The old woman never enquired about the food or writing paraphernalia. I was a little bit dismayed by her lack of interest, but no big deal, this was just her personality, so I had to deal with it. As she turned, I noticed white dust on the back of her dress. And then I saw it! The old woman had been lying on the bench, the bench with the map. The map was gone! The old woman must have tossed and turned in her sleep, wiping the chalk clean off the bench. My godsend had been stolen away, erased, and my shortcut home gone forever. I was brimming with anger. My face must have turned ten shades of purple. I was infuriated and stared daggers in the back of the old woman for several second and then stopped. My head about to explode, I was speechless, and then all the air escaped from my balloon. Now I was thoroughly depressed. Like all the life had been sucked out of my soul. What had she done? What am I going to do now?

I asked her if she had noticed the drawing on the bench before she lay down. She shook her head and looked at me if I was crazy. Maybe she thought I had been seeing things, with the heat, exhaustion, all the stress, you know. I related the story of the map and what I saw. She had little reaction once again. I had the impression she did not believe a word I was telling her. Her attitude was getting me more wound up. She must be too old to care, who knows. She must know I was not happy, but this didn't seem to bother her at all. I shook my head in disbelief, and she turned away continuing to look out the porthole.

This was obviously an accident, but I felt like screaming. Would not have done any good, but I would have felt better, I think. She would have not damaged the map purposely. She had no idea, it was there, or was just too tired to pay attention. I should have told her, warned her, did something to alert her, but I did nothing. Maybe I deserve this for not paying attention to details, important details. Unfortunately, at this moment, I found it extremely difficult to forgive her for this costly error. I really had many mixed emotions, all bad, and all aimed at the old woman. I may never get home now...never!

I believed in my heart I had found a fast way home, but I guess there is no fast way home. Now I really had to count on the old woman and that made me extremely uncomfortable. Seemed like my life was in the hands of another, someone who really didn't care if I got home or not. What a position...what a tragedy.

I was sad, but conceded. Remaining angry would not accomplish anything. Better to forgive and forget...something I have never been able to do. Either one was not going to be easy, not my nature.

Sitting there, feeling sorry for myself, I remembered the time my mother gave away my baseball card collection to a local charity at Christmas. She had found my collector's album in a box, on a shelf in the garage. I hadn't played with them, used them, or looked at them for over two years. She presumed I was tired of them and didn't want them anymore. On the afternoon of Christmas Eve, she packed them up along with several other boxes of things and took them to the local charity. I was totally unaware my sacred collection had danced out the door.

Several days later she remembered and then told me. I went crazy, threw a tantrum, and told my mother I would never forgive her for what she had done. I really didn't forgive her, not even up to today. Those were my cards whether I played with them or not, and no one else was allowed to have them. My mom tried to explain, but I wouldn't listen, I didn't care what her reasons were for what she did. When she had enough, she sent me to my room for acting so stupid. I am sure she thought she didn't have to ask me because moms are permitted to do whatever they want. That's the feeling I had, "mother's privilege" prevails and nothing

I can say of do about it. I slammed the door and never came out for dinner. Even today, I still want my cards back, and I am still angry. That was a few years ago, but I still don't feel like forgiving my mom, even though she apologized for not asking me before giving away the set. Big deal, the damage was done...no apology will ever fix it. That's just me.

The old lady turned and muttered something. She had found the original trail. This was her peace offering of sorts, so we decided it best to set off. Good news I guess. I looked at her, and again mentioned the map. She pulled at her clothes and noticed the chalk dust on the back of her dress. She looked at me sheepishly and turned away stepping towards the makeshift elevator. I believe she felt bad even though I could not really tell. She was a hard person to read. I told her it was okay, and we'll find our way home. She showed no expression as she boarded the platform and, I lowered us both to the valley floor. I knew it would take hours for the red flush to leave my face and the anger to subside. Exercise might be the answer, so a brisk walk might be beneficial. No shortage of that on this never ending treadmill.

She pointed ahead and I followed. What else could I do. I took one final look at the stoic tree. High in the branches I was sure I saw a blue jay moving its head from side to side. I shaded my eyes and strained to see through the sunlight, then the silhouette flew out of the cover and off around the hillside. Maybe the map was not what I thought, who really knows. Maybe just all in my mind because I wanted to get home so badly. The map might have taken us in the wrong direction, who knows. I'll use this analogy to help sooth my soul. What's done is done, get on with it!

The old woman lead the way knowing we would soon meet up with the original path, apparent our journey far from over. I walked backwards for a bit staring at the tree, marveling at its greatness, and then suddenly, the Voice.

"FORGIVENESS must be practiced with a true and sincere heart. FORGIVENESS is one important means of healing ourselves and healing our relationship with others, expressing kindness, and is an ongoing and lifelong process."

"A wise man once said, "If we practice an eye for an eye and a tooth for a tooth, the whole world would soon be blind and toothless." It takes courage to forgive and self forgiveness enables us to release guilt, shame, pride, or the illusion we are perfect. FORGIVENESS does not change the past, but enlarges the future. "To err is human, to forgive divine." FORGIVENESS is a great power.

Fading...fading...gone. Just like before. What's the point? Thank you Voice for more of the same! Nice to hear from you, but I need directions and help. Can you give me this? Which way to go and how soon will I get there, is all I really want to hear. I was obviously agitated by the day's events and not in the mood for another pointless blurb. Frustration had gotten the better of me. This was all too much to bear.

SEVEN

The Rock

We marched on, and within a very short time, found our path which had been broken apart, and hidden within the depths of the small valley. The old woman seemed to be back on track, so I stayed close at hand keeping a look out for anything that may hinder or help. I reassured her that I was no longer upset about the map because maybe it wasn't really a map. Maybe the directions had nothing to do with where I needed to go, and we could have ended up worse off. I told the old woman I trusted her more than any map because she undoubtedly knew her way home. I was not sure if my ploy had worked because as usual, she did not show any real expression. I assumed she really did not care what I thought, being confident in her own abilities. She knew the way and I didn't, advantage old woman. I had to put a lot of faith in her right now. She was all the help I had, and I was thankful for that.

After a few hours we stopped, sat on some boulders and rested. We ate the berries I had found this morning and I could not get that tree-house out of my mind. Even more amazing was how I found it. Just about got killed, probably should have been killed. I love trees, they give us oxygen, give us life, saved my life. Trees are great.

We had been sitting for a while when I began to notice a strange dimness start to settle upon the area. I glanced upwards noting the clear blue sky, void of any clouds whatsoever. Really weird, the sun seemed so bright. Where was this dimness coming from? The old woman stood as she began to notice the same thing, I believe. I stood as well and looked in every direction.

Now the expression on the old woman's face was pronounced and displayed a note of worry. Odd, because up until now, she was never one to display much emotion. Seeing this caused me obvious concern. My sixth sense was not really in tune with the universe, but maybe hers was. Just had to wait it out, wait and see, hope whatever it was would blow over. I had enough to deal with, just get me out of "Weirdo Land", I want to go home. The old woman crept slowly to the path, observing all around her. She looked up, down, then quickly behind as if to catch someone or something off guard. I followed, hoping everything was alright. The old woman appeared agitated and on edge. No idea what concern would make her this nervous. The unexplained dimness intensified and the old woman stopped in her tracks, eyes wide open.

An eerie silence shrouded the area. I couldn't put my finger on it, but I had the feeling someone or something was following us. From her reaction, the old woman must have had the exact same feeling or one even stronger. Strange shadows were now prevalent everywhere, morphing into a potpourri shapes and sizes as we watched. We slowly moved along the path. I tried to focus on the way, but these shadows had become quite a distraction. Now the shadows were forming images of an intimidating nature, fangs, horns, claws and the like. They would come and go, shrink and grow at their whim. If I didn't know better, I would have thought these pesky penumbras were trying to prevent our advance, or discourage our progress, in order to convince us of taking an alternative route. I should have totally ignored them because what can a shadow do anyway, not much, I think. Definitely, something was up, and it wasn't good.

The shadows would no relent, in fact, seemed to increase in numbers. I felt like we were being

69

surrounded. Just the sunlight playing with the forest I thought, so chalk the sightings up to fatigue and lack of food. From time to time I sneaked a peek behind to try and discover the source, but found no logical explanation for any shadow to even be there. I must be hallucinating. More and more, like a marching army, the shadows began to crowd around us, corralling us like wild horses.

Then I heard several unusual guttural sounds, like someone gurgling. I glanced over at the old woman to see if she noticed as well. Her face was contorted, hands waving frantically in the air. She was spinning slowly in circles. She was making me dizzy. I watched and quickly realized, the sounds were coming form her. I worried she might be on the verge of a seizure and go into convulsions. Her eyes were bulging and she was starting to scare me more than the shadows. She began to murmur something of which I could not hear clearly. Sounded like a chant or some sort of incantation. She kept repeating the same words and sounds then suddenly growled loudly, like a wild animal. Yikes, I prayed she was not going to turn into a werewolf or vampire and slaughter me. I started to tremble, the anticipation harrowing beyond belief. The old woman turned her back to me and let out an excruciating, high pitched squeal. I covered my ears and ducked as the armada of shadows seemed to go crazy, racing and dive bombing at light speed. The shadows seemed to be screaming as well, screaming in pain. The ear shattering assault was unbearable. I was closed my eyes for a split second, then silence.

In the wink of an eye, the shadows disappeared. I looked around, nothing. I thought it best not to say a word. The shadows were super creepy, and I was glad they were gone. At least I hoped they were. But maybe what just happened with the old woman was even creepier. I told myself to forget it, don't question it, I must accept, and file for future reference, no explanation needed. Where ever I was, weirdness seemed to be the order of the day, the norm for now. Get used to it!

Thanks to the old woman, the shadows had definitely made a permanent departure, so we continued on and soon entered a clearing. The ground formation in this vicinity seemed out of the ordinary. The entire area appeared to be dotted with giant pieces of slate. I could see up ahead, the pattern continuing for some distance. Like a park filled with giant stepping stones. Interesting natural phenomena I thought.

The old woman pointed to the ground and signaled for me to follow her, so I did. Then she abruptly stopped and listened. I heard a faint rumble and then smelled rotten eggs, sulfur. The rumble began building momentum, louder and louder. The old woman stood still and motioned for me to do similar. I waited.

The rumblings increased and then a loud hissing sound prevailed. Like a whale shooting water out its blowhole, the earth began to do the same. We found ourselves imprisoned in a field of geysers. Steam spewed continuously as the boiling spring water exploded through the earth holes, high into the air.

The water show would have been spectacular from a distance, but we were caught right in the middle of the performance, no telling when it would end, or whether we would be steamed to death or boiled alive. I wasn't sure if the old woman had a cure or a spell for this one. I was beginning to wonder about her. Who was this old woman?

To be so close was frightening, having no idea when and where the next one would come from, maybe right beneath us. No use to try and time the eruptions, or run between them, best to stay put as the old woman

71

instructed. We were held captive for what seemed like an eternity. Finally, the rumbles subsided and the geysers took a breather. The old woman waved frantically at me to start moving, so I did, quickly. The old woman seemed to have a well polished sense of timing, or maybe a keen sense of hearing that allowed her to forecast their arrival. In any event, without her I might have been scalded, seriously injured, or worse if caught out here by myself. I told myself to never complain about the old woman slowing me down, or being a burden. She may turn out to be a real life saver, maybe already has.

Now free from the large slate plates, we continued onward. It wasn't long after we came upon an unassuming waterfall, and seemingly a dead end. The area was cool and the spray refreshing. I filled my container with fresh drinking water and was thankful for that. The old woman took a seat on a log beside the tiny stream, removed her sandals, and dipped her feet into the cool water. Good idea, so I did the same. It felt invigorating, great. We both relaxed and enjoyed the peaceful setting, but I was a little worried because there seemed no way to proceed, no path to follow, no where to go. The woman slipped back into her sandals and stood up. I followed suit and waited for her lead.

She cautiously navigated the slippery rocks around the front of the waterfall and slid in behind the curtain of cascading water. I hurried to catch up, careful with the footing. Once behind, I found the old woman at the entrance to a cave-like tunnel which the waterfall had kept well concealed. I smiled. My confidence in the old woman was building.

The dampness provided a welcome cover from the afternoon heat, and the sound of the falls had a very calming effect. The tunnel was quite wide and long, and I could see light far up ahead.

Light at the end of the tunnel, I could only dream that would be the case, home at last, wishful thinking. I almost wished the tunnel would not end...it was actually nice in here. I noticed several outlines along the tunnel wall, possibly drawings of some sort, hard to make out in the semi-darkness. I thought I saw a mountain, a wall, and some animal with many heads. Who knows, impossible to tell, could be something totally different. Oh well, all good things must end. Finally, we reached the exit, and back into the blinding sunlight. Without hesitation or breaking stride we continued side by side.

Another hour or so passed, and we came to the top of a knoll. The grassy area was embedded with stone markers of some kind, all shapes and sizes. I noticed some markings on the stones, but could not decipher the text. The old woman was careful where to step, and directed me to do the same, but I did not know why. Possibly this was some sort of sacred place, or burial ground, just guessing. The old woman must know this place, so I obeyed her instructions. Negotiating the markers with caution, I felt a strange sensation of hot and cold. I became jittery and weak in the knees. This possibly the result of some magnetic force field or other phenomena unique to the area. Suddenly, a small shadow darted past and I looked up to see what I thought was a blue jay whiz by. The nervous feelings subsided. Managing to side step all the stones, we grinded to a halt.

A huge monolith was half buried in the hillside. The stone was intriguing, like something you would find on Easter Island, maybe not that prolific. I walked around in front to observe the obscure markings covered from view by the tall grass. I wanted to touch them, but the old woman stopped me immediately. She shook her head, an ominous warning. I took heed. She must have been here before or know what the inscription meant. I would not question her insight, hands off. I have to admit I was acutely curious. Maybe the text could help us in some way, maybe not, stop dreaming and pay attention.

Far below, in the distance, I could see a small valley with a forked roadway. The old woman pointed at both, so I could not determine which one was the correct one. I could see a sign post in the middle of the fork. I needed to get a closer look to determine the proper route.

I was about to head down the hill when I saw a young boy, maybe my age, emerge from around the corner of the forested area. He stopped at the sign post, looking for some time. A few seconds later, three other youths appeared from the cover of the bushes and approached him very calmly. One boy from the group bumped into the boy who was looking at the sign post. I witnessed another boy from the group, pick the traveller's pocket and pass the contents to the third boy. They moved calmly along as if nothing happened. The traveller seemed unaware anything sinister had occurred. The victim stayed at the crossroads for a while, then started down the road.

I was somewhat surprised, and at the same time bothered by what had just taken place, so I motioned to the old woman to stay here. I rambled down the hillside in the direction of the threesome. I caught up with them in minutes and they were surprised to see me. Not too many visitors out in the middle of nowhere. This group of pickpockets was slick and well rehearsed, like something out of Oliver Twist. They were quite startled, but three against one gave them the advantage. They lined up, folding their arms across their chests, giving me a though look. Not sure what they expected. They said nothing. I hid my uneasiness and thought what have I got myself into? What am I going to so now? The standoff continued, so I finally felt inclined to break the ice and toss in my two cents worth.

I said I saw what they did and demanded they return the wallet. They all laughed and slapped each other on the shoulders. They denied taking anything, but I could see the wallet sticking out of one of the boy's pockets. The wallet was unique and colourful. They said it was theirs. I threatened to report them and they burst out laughing once again. They treated my intrusion as some kind of joke and they were going to have the last laugh. Report to whom? Who was I? They were not fazed by my bravado. I tried to stay in character, tough and unrelenting. Not easy considering I was probably going to be attacked and pummeled. I thought I would play it out, inwardly praying for an easy and favourable outcome.

The trio thought themselves bullet proof and were building confidence. I had to try another tactic. I told them I had just come from a village and I would return and report them to the local authorities. Now they started to pay attention.

I continued, saying the authorities would contact their parents and the entire village would know about their activities. I stressed their families would suffer the humiliation and embarrassment of such a revelation.

They were really listening now. I thought I had them on the run. I again demanded the return of the wallet. They looked at one another and burst into laughter once again. I was running out of ideas and had no real way to convince them to give back the wallet. I sensed they knew I was short on ammunition, my verbal attack sounding pretty hollow.

They knew I was not a local, and had probably nothing to fear, their word against mine. Actually, I had no idea where they lived, but most likely not too far away. They definitely held the advantage and it would really take a stroke of genius to have things turn my way. I gave them a tough look and said I was only going to give them one more chance. More snickers, then suddenly an uncharacteristic silence from all three. Their eyes seemed to go right past me, above me, through me. They were looking at something behind me. For some unknown reason they seemed worried, even frightened if I had to guess. What was going on? What were they looking at? What had changed their arrogant mood? How strange. I turned slightly, followed their line of sight, and received my answer.

Sitting atop the tomb-like boulder like a meditating monk, was the old woman. The tall grass covered the face of the stone, so from this distance she seemed to be floating on air in the lotus position. I turned back to the boys who were obviously spooked. They could not take their eyes of the vision. In many rural areas, superstitions run rampant and are part of the cultures. I heard them whisper to each other without their eyes breaking away from the old woman for a second. I heard their mutterings. They claimed the old woman must be a witch as no other could float on air. She must be here to practice her spells and may decide to use them for fun. The thought of being turned into a toad, field mouse, or other, did not seem to sit well with boys. They were not so aggressive now, more on the defensive, awaiting the witch's next move. Frozen, the boys kept a close watch just in case.

Opportunity at hand, I told the boys the old woman was my friend and we were travelling together. Mouths agape, now I had their full attention. They could plainly see I was not frightened. Why not? I should be just as startled as them? I needed to prove what I had just said, show them I was telling the truth. I was sure the boys were asking themselves many questions. Like how they were going to escape and avoid certain disaster.

I turned and waved to the old woman, she responded in a same manner. I turned and grinned confidently. No fear written on my face. This should be evidence enough, time to make a deal.

Their eyes bulged, jaws dropped, and I could smell the fear. I trashed talk about spells and being turned into creepy crawlies and other unsightly creatures. Then I said nothing. The boys kept looking at me then back up at the old woman. The trio began whispering amongst themselves. I sensed their obvious discomfort. Their confidence shattered, I thought it an opportune time to request the wallet again. This time there was no hesitation. The wallet was handed over and I strongly suggested the trio leave the area while they still had a chance. The three boys ran like the wind, disappearing into the forest. I turned back to the old woman and showed the wallet. She maintained her place. I shrugged my shoulders and looked for the victim. I saw him quite far down the road, so I thought I better hustle after him.

I caught up with the boy and presented the wallet. He was shocked and reaching into his pocket was surprised to find nothing. Surprisingly he then began to accuse me of stealing it. I tried to reason with him. If I stole it, why would I return it? I told him to check the contents, so he did. He finally realized everything was there, all his money untouched. He still seemed a little unsure on what to make of all this, stunned I guess, that he had been violated so easily.

I asked if he knew the way and he said he did not. He appeared angry and not in the helpful mood. Guess I don't blame him, but I could not force him to assist. I could only hope the old woman knew the correct road to take. I headed back to the fork in the road to see if I could determine the right course.

The old woman was now standing by the signage. The base had been twisted and the shingles were pointing in no specific direction. The old woman shook her head. This was a bad sign. Going off on the wrong road could be disastrous, we could be lost forever. I thought the woman knew the area. I guess she depended on the sign as well. Having to take an educated guess, or flipping a coin was not what I had in mind. We looked at each other, perplexed. Where was the Voice when I needed it.

Then I heard it, a voice, the voice of the youth who had just been robbed. He had come back and advised us the boys must have damaged the sign to cause a diversion.

Obviously this had been a cunning plan to take advantage of passersby who were unfamiliar with the locality. He said he was born near here and the road we needed to take was the one on the right. I had to believe him even though a few minutes ago he seemed reluctant to help. I thanked him and would now be able to continue our journey. I was hopeful the old woman would recognize the way eventually, and that would be a great comfort.

I stood there in silence, and thought back to a time when I was playing soccer with a group of neighbourhood kids. We were playing in a vacant lot sandwiched between two older homes. The game went on for some time and the score was tied. Rick's mom had just yelled from the bottom of the street, dinner was ready. I knew the game would end very soon, it was Rick's ball. I was very competitive, good at all sports, and always wanted to win. As Rick whistled an end to the game, I became frustrated. I had the ball right in front of the opponent's goal. I kicked the ball as hard as I could and it sailed over the goal and into the neighbour's yard, shattering the basement window.

Everyone ran away to avoid confronting the owner.

I was worried all evening, thinking the neighbour would come to my house. Maybe he had seen who kicked the ball? I knew my parents would be very angry at me for breaking the window. They might even have to pay for a new one, and take the money out of my allowance. No way, I thought. I will just sit and wait it out, but the wait was scary. I just went to may room and stayed there for the rest of the night, fearing that knock on the door. It never came.

The next day, I walked past the vacant lot and saw Rick and his father repairing the window. I had no idea why. How did the owner know it was us, unless he saw what happened or someone had told him. No one came to my home, so I assumed no one saw me kick the ball through the window. Yet, Rick was right there and his dad did not look happy. I was never invited back to play soccer with those boys, and really had no idea why not until I heard from someone in school. The soccer ball had Rick's name on it, so the owner paid a visit to Rick's parents. I can only imagine Rick had owned up to being responsible and never implicated me as the culprit. He took it on the chin and never squealed. I was certain his parents had issued an equitable punishment, one I deserved, not Rick. I should have came forward, immediately or shortly after at least, but chose to abstain and let someone else take the blame. After all, it was an accident. I didn't mean it, only a window. No big deal, right?

Then the silence was broken. The Voice was here again.

"HONESTY is the foundation of the right action, the truth. Honesty is comprised of communicating in an honest and rigorous manner, as well as possessing integrity, which is being truthful, keeping our word. We must be truthful not only in word, but in our actions as well. This is truly the law of the Universe. Lying is seen as a form of weakness and brings with it, dishonour. Veracity or sincerity may also be considered as a form of honesty."

"HONESTY gives us the foundation to do things to the best of our ability."

The Voice vanished like a wisp of wind. Nothing to say and no help as usual. We had to be on our way without delay. No use waiting around for next useless revelation.

EIGHT

The Oasis

NO TIME LIKE THE PRESENT I ALWAYS SAY. I lead the way as the trail was now well defined. The raw wilderness endless, we went about our business, keeping the straight and narrow. Wow! Never knew the earth had this many trees and such massive, wide open spaces. We were pretty much out of everything, no food, no more water, nothing. I should have conserved more of our supplies. I sure hoped the old woman could locate some more berries like this morning. Mom always prepared our meals. They were always there, on time, when we were hungry. I never gave a thought as to how much effort went into putting all those dishes together, three times each day. Buying the groceries, choosing the ingredients, preparing the meat, vegetables, and potatoes, and making them taste great. What a job. I never appreciated the effort before now. Everything was laid out in front of me on the table to enjoy. I never lifted a finger, never thought I had to. I wouldn't mind helping put together a meal now, you better believe it. Oh well, dream on.

I motored along forgetting my companion may be not so quick of foot. I looked behind to check on her and she was gone. What now?I panicked for a second. Had she taken a turn I had missed, and left me alone going in the wrong direction? Had one of the forest predators dragged her off into the underbrush? I didn't need this. I ran back searching everywhere, yelling and screaming for her to appear. I slashed the bushes and branches with my staff, pounding the tree trunks to draw her attention. What could have happened? This is just great. Maybe she is angry at me because of the tree house incident and decided to leave me to my own ambitions. After all, she said she knew the way, and I sure didn't. Where is she?

I continued to rant and rave, scurrying in all directions like a madman. Out of the corner of my eye, I spotted someone emerge from the thick foliage, thank God, the old woman. A sigh of relief ensued, but I was definitely upset she would wander off like that without warning. Could have been the death of her...or me! Maybe I should have been paying more attention, maybe it was my fault. She wasn't lost, that was the good news, and I saw her carrying something in her baggy dress. She proudly showed me more berries and some delicious looking mushrooms. Placing the mushrooms in her oversized pocket, we shared some berries and a moment of rest. I needed the break to recover from my near heart attack.

We felt much better after the break and ready to move on. I guess we were now back on even terms, so I felt good about that. After another hour or so, I felt something was different, the air. All the humidity was quickly vanishing, but I had no idea why. The trees were becoming sparse and soon there were none. The ground broke apart easily when stepped on, not firm. What lie before us was a vast wasteland. This barren expanse was a virtual desert, with tiny gusts of wind whipping up the sandy floor. I looked at the woman. I could see for miles, the horizon giving no indication of direction, no point in the distance to use as a guide.

What's that... why now? Miles and miles of baking hot sand, good God! She pointed straight ahead. I could only hope she knew where she was going because I saw nothing but an invisible road to nowhere. I stood there staring out into this endless frontier. Now I had to put all my trust in the old woman's sense of direction.

No choice, I had to follow. We set off across the

badlands. I had an uncomfortable feeling in the pit of my stomach. Maybe the discomfort was just from the lack of food. No, it was something a lot worse...something out there...I could feel it.

I was certain we had covered many miles as my feet were stinging from the effects of the sandy terrain. Like walking along the beach barefoot, you can only take so much. Like a hamster on a treadmill, it always feels like you are taking two steps forward and one step back. I hated that. Obviously, this was not the place to be without water, and I was positive we would not exactly be running into any rivers or lakes out here, dry as a bone. The old woman laboured along side, but never made a sound, finding the footing a real challenge. She proved to be a real trooper. I just hoped she wouldn't pass out or die on me, this was tough sledding even for me.

The heat and exhaustion were starting to wear me down and I had to stop. There was no place to sit, the sand was too hot. My skin was turning a cooked lobster red and was starting to tighten up. The heat rippled off the sandy surface in waves and I guessed the temperature was over a hundred degrees Fahrenheit. Incredible! Just another day at the beach...just maybe the meanest beach on earth.

We struggled onward. Finally, I thought I saw something in the distance, something green, possibly vegetation. I hoped this was not a mirage or some other form of optical phenomena. The heat rising from the sandy soil and the refraction of light in the desert can play tricks on your mind, especially when you are exhausted and dehydrated. The old woman also saw the same thing, indicating so by making a drinking motion. If she really knew this place, she must believe, or know there will be water up ahead. Her signal energized me and I was confident our thirst would be quenched.

I dragged my tired legs through the sand, and about thirty minutes later we arrived at an area resembling a type of oasis. What a comforting sight. The greenery lead me to believe there must be water here somewhere, hopefully not all underground. Every oasis has water, right? The small palm trees provided some much needed shade, so we sat on the tufts of grass for awhile to catch our breath. My throat was extremely dry, and I was feeling a little dizzy. I am sure the old woman felt similar or worse.

I did not want to move, but we had to find the water, it must be here. I looked over at the old woman who was justifiably exhausted, in no rush to move.

I struggled to my feet, not letting on I was ready to drop. I had to remain strong as a morale booster for the old woman. I couldn't let her down. I was hoping her village was on the other side of this wasteland, but she never mentioned it. No point I guess, we'll be there when we get there. Now let's find the water.

Fifteen minutes into the search, I heard the old woman yelp. I hurried over to her location and there it was, she had found the watering hole. The old woman smiled, pretty proud of herself, so was I. Fresh drinking water...a gift from heaven. She still had the container I had gotten from the fruit vendor and knelt down near the edge of ground well. With container in hand, she leaned forward, ready to fill the canteen with the desert's gift.

Suddenly, I heard an unusual sound. The old woman stopped. We both looked around thinking we might be just hearing things, desert things. Then again, so I knew I heard someone say something. It was a muffled sound, but a speaking voice for sure. Where was it coming from? Who was making the sound? We both scouted around, but could not locate the source. Then we heard it again. We looked at each other and shrugged our shoulders. The old woman was about to try again when we heard a definite, "No!" The old woman backed off and staggered to her feet. We panned the area again, then I saw movement out of the corner of my eye.

Looking to my right, I noticed a figure, a human figure. From behind a row of granite boulders, heavily bandaged from head to toe, the figure hoisted itself upright using the rocks for support. I was shocked to say the least. The cloth wrappings were filthy and tattered, exposing lesions and horrid discolourations on the skin. I didn't know what to make of this, but the old woman did. The old woman screamed at the top of her lungs.

"Leper...leper...leper!"

I covered my ears, her bellowing so intense. She backed away quickly and held up the container in a defensive position. Scared out of her wits, she was trembling from head to toe. She began waving the canteen, then swiping the air in front of her, akin to swatting flies. Fearful of attack, the old woman began murmuring and hissing. The mummy-like figure struggled to maintain its balance while making its advance. The old woman growled, but the leper stood fast. His face was totally covered with the exception of an eye space allowing him to see clearly.

His eyes were hypnotic in a sense, a dark, piercing, emerald green. I couldn't help but look. A memorable physical trait, one I would not soon forget. I turned to look at the old woman, and he put up his hand as a gesture not to hurt him. His voice was weak, but he spoke in a calm manner, his words clear.

He related to us that the watering hole was now contaminated, poisoned. He limped over to the edge of the spring, holding up one hand to ward off any form of aggression from the old woman. Methodically, he kicked at the surrounding grass. His weather beaten boots lifted up small bone fragments. He pointed to the skeletal remains of the many victims, hidden along its perimeter. He was right, the water was undrinkable, and most likely fatal. Shocked and dismayed, I thanked him for stopping us. Drinking this water would have been suicidal.

He could have easily stayed out of sight, let us fill our container, and then watched us die, but he did not. I had nothing to offer him except a few berries and a couple of raw mushrooms. He nodded, took the offering, and then a seat on the boulders. He nibbled away in silence, staring at the ground, never looking in our direction. The old woman backed up further. She wanted no part of this, but for some reason, I was not afraid, and I could sense his pain. Normally not very empathetic, actually not empathetic at all, I felt a compassionate connection. That's a new one.

An outcast of society in many cultures, lepers conjured up fear amongst the ignorant. I did not feel the like this, however the old woman fit the stereotypical mode. I couldn't really blame her, he did look awfully intimidating.

I am sure she had seen what was under the bandages at one point in her life, a sight one could not easily forget. I had no intention of letting my imagination run with that one. I shut it down immediately. Reality bites, but the math was simple. Without water, what were we to do? What are we going to do now?

The oasis spread over several acres in all directions. There was lots of vegetation, all sorts. I suggested we look for food and water and the leper agreed. The old woman just put her hand in front of her face. I told here to stay here and I would go to search, but she refused to stay any where near the leper. It was imperative we find another source. Finally, I decided we should all go since the food and water was for everyone. The old woman walked far off to the side and the leper limped along behind.

The oasis was an interesting place. In one area I did find some form of cacti, but not the kind that could hold much water, probably none. The broad flat paddle skin looked too thick to penetrate with any instrument and the needles were a major deterrent. Not worth the effort. We eventually spotted a cluster of small trees, fig trees. This was a pleasant surprise. Figs were tasty and nutritious, and hopefully full of juicy nectar.

Not a hundred feet away stood a lone coconut tree. Not sure exactly what kind of oasis this was, furnished with figs and a solitary coconut tree, but I was grateful they were here. Maybe we could survive the night, divine intervention favouring us at the moment. The old woman gathered the figs from the low lying branches while the leper and I were going to try our luck with the coconuts.

I stood at the base of the tree looking up, about ten metres I guessed. I searched for some rocks and tried to knock them down. I was a good shot and hit them all except they would not fall. I didn't like the next course of action, but time to practice my tree climbing skills. I took off my shoes and started my ascent. I remembered seeing how the natives in Polynesia climbed the coconut trees, like a clever monkey. The technique worked well as I made my way up the tree fairly easily and in reach of the nuts. I looked down, big mistake, I hated heights. Vertigo got the best of me and I felt faint immediately, so I looked out across the oasis to clear my mind.

The intense heat rippled the desert air making things worse not better. Back to the business at hand, the coconuts. I disconnected the pods and dropped them to the ground shouting "bonsai!"

The leper kept his distance and I could see the old woman had stopped to observe. As the each coconut was launched downwards, the old woman made a frantic "slam dunk" motion. If I didn't know better, I would guess she wanted me to plunk the leper. I was surprised at her hostility towards a person who minutes ago had possibly saved her life. I didn't really get it, but she remained animated as each of the five coconuts hit the earth. The leper's watchful eye had also spotted the old woman's antics and no doubt, under all that armour boiled a red hot leper. Trouble in paradise I suspect. Great...this is all I need.

Job well done, time to descend. This should be fun...not! The rough tree bark was blistering my feet. I had to be careful not to contract any open wounds, a ton more walking to come. I made it down and collected the bounty. I had noticed a nice grassy area from the top of the tree, so I signaled the old woman to follow. I dumped the coconuts to the ground and the old woman arrived with a load of figs. I fumbled around for something to smash open the nuts when I heard the old woman scream once again, ear shattering. Gave me the willies...yikes...she should be an opera singer...good thing no windows around.

I turned to see the leper yielding a large curved blade. He raised it over his head and brought it down on the skull shaped nut.

"CRACK!"

The nut split open. I rushed to pick it up before all the precious liquid had escaped. I offered the first drink to the old woman and she gulped it down. I then handed it to the leper, the old woman backing away from the immediate area.

He hesitated; seemingly surprised he would be honoured with the next sip. He took the nut in his hand and drank. I held out my hand as a signal for him to give me the blade. He surrendered the weapon and I cracked open another nut. We ate and drank as the sun set and desert began to cool. I kept the blade with me so the old woman would feel more comfortable. The leper seemed to have no problem with that arrangement.

Bellies full, or as full as they could be on figs, coconut meat, and coconut juice, I decided it was time to close my weary eyes. Hoped the others would follow suit. The march through the desert was a killer, every muscle in my body ached. Climbing up and down a coconut tree didn't help either.

Nightfall was upon us, and we all found our own suitable spots to retire. The old woman set down quite a distance from the two of us. I warned her to stay closer but she refused. Deserts were notorious for creatures of the night, scorpions, snakes and the like, but she would not listen. Apparently her fear of the leper was not going to subside any time soon. I only hoped when we set off in the morning she would feel more comfortable, just the two of us once again. I organized my sleeping spot, checking for little creatures, hoping nothing larger considered this little piece of paradise their happy hunting ground. I assumed many animals would usually come to the oasis to drink, but their instincts should have already warned them the water here was contaminated, so hopefully they would keep their distance. We all took our places and lay down for the night. The air was fresh and the oasis peaceful. I was looking forward to a good night's rest. No reason to think otherwise. As soon as my head hit the fluffy grass pillow, I was out like a light.

My visit to dreamland was short-lived. I heard the old woman screaming hysterically. She was somewhere in the darkness so I jumped my feet, got my bearings, and listened for direction. It was pitch black, and I could not see much, but I knew approximately how far she had camped from us. I noticed the leper was gone, not a good sign. I feared the worst and rushed over to the spot the old woman had selected for the night. In the moonlight, I could see the leper standing over the old woman holding a large rock above his head. Something was dripping from the rock...blood.

I looked down at the old woman who lay there motionless, blood splattered all over her face. I could not believe this was happening. The leper staggered backwards and the old woman began to stir, she was alive. I knelt down to examine the old woman, illumination provided by the full moon. She was regaining consciousness and mumbling in delirium. I had no medical supplies and the scene looked serious. My heart thumping, I had no idea what to do. Her eyes popped open, her straight ahead stare frightening.

Surprisingly, she sat upright and looked at me. I was in shock. I thought she was near death's door. Placing my hand on her shoulder to help balance her position, I began to take note of the surrounding area.

The old woman had laid down, her head next to a large stone. On the stone I saw the remains of a snake, a large poisonous snake, a viper of some sort. The reptile had been crushed beyond recognition, its blood everywhere. I glanced up at the leper, the rock, and the old woman. Like Sherlock Holmes, I used my power of deduction to conclude the leper had killed the snake, with no intention of harming the old woman.

He had saved her life. He must have been watching over us knowing the possible dangers. I had his blade, so he used the rock to save the old woman. The leper dropped the bloody stone and slowly moved away, back into the darkness. I comforted the old woman who was still traumatized. She also thought the leper was about to kill her, or at least make the attempt. She had no idea the snake was only inches away, its lethal fangs poised to deliver the death strike. I wiped the blood from her face using some water from the canister and a cloth I found in the pocket of her dress. She told me the leper had tried to kill her. Truly convinced of this fallacy, she refused to believe the truth, until I showed her the remains of the snake. She looked at me and then in the direction of the retreating leper. She said nothing, but her eyes said a lot, full of anger and hatred as I read it, still not convinced.

Even though the evidence was clear, I had an overwhelming suspicion her thinking could not be altered at this particular moment, maybe never. After several minutes, she began to settle down, taking a closer look at scene. She stood up, steadied herself, than I assisted her in finding another suitable place to rest. With her appearing more comfortable, I lumbered back to my resting spot and we all tried to go back to sleep, little chance of that. Who knew what else was out there, morning could not come soon enough. I felt more exhausted now than before. I closed my eyes but sleep was the farthest thing from my mind. I'd better keep one eye open tonight I thought, the fun might not be over.

The leper seemed to be able to go back to sleep without reservation. The old woman, hard to say, and myself, could merely hope to get some much needed rest. Too much excitement I guess. This was the longest night of my life, but somewhere in the middle of it, I dozed off.

As soon as the sun began to rise, I got up. Maybe we should leave early while the sun was not so hot. I could see the old woman already up, pacing in the distance. Not sure exactly what she was doing, but she seemed okay. The leper was sitting on a rock looking at the ground, kind of dejected I presumed considering the night's events. I cracked open the rest of the coconuts and distributed the juice equally amongst the three of us, giving some refreshment to the leper, and taking some over to the old woman who still refused to join us. I divided and delivered the figs in the same manner and shortly thereafter, we were ready to leave. Gathering our belongings, the old woman and I began our departure.

The leper began to follow. The old woman stopped. There was no way he was tagging along she thought. I had no idea he wanted to join us, but I guess I was wrong. Every step we took, he took. Frustration set in, like a ping pong game gone bad, back and forth, who would win, nobody for sure in this case.

Sweat dripped from my brow into my eyes. I could feel the tension, and the stress mounting. I didn't need this but had to deal with it. I looked away from both of them towards the grove of fig trees and noticed my little friend the blue jay, bobbing his little head up and down. Where did he come from? I wiped away the sweat with my shirt sleeve and looked again, the blue jay was gone. Could it have been a mirage? Was the blue jay acknowledging what I was about to do? Did he already know? This bird is really smart, because I didn't. After several moments of contemplation, I directed my attention back to the problem at hand. I knew what to do, and it would not be a popular decision. Think before you speak. I reminded myself of this several times, but before I could get a word out, something obscure came to mind.

Once again, deep in thought, I drifted back, finding myself outside the shopping mall. Three large specially equipped transport vans stopped near the front entrance.

Teams of people emerged and began unloading people in wheelchairs, walkers, and the like. Easily identified, these mentally and physically handicapped individuals had already endured a lifelong struggle, and it seemed apparent there would be no solution to their suffering.

The entourage paraded into the mall and I thought...why? Why bring them here? No one wants to look at this? Take them somewhere else, please. I was going to go into the mall but changed my mind, ruined my whole day. I had no sympathy, empathy, no feeling whatsoever. The position I took was, as long as it's not me, why should I care, why should I feel anything towards these people. I had no conception of what it would be like to be in that position or be that person. I had absolutely no compassion for their plight, not my problem. Out of sight, out of mind, seemed the best policy under these circumstances.

I never thought myself fortunate to be the way I am, I just thought that is the way it was supposed to be, I deserve at least this. I did not understand why anyone would want to spend their time looking after these kinds of people when they could be doing something else. What a waist of time. I guess they were getting paid a lot of money to attend to these people. I was wrong. The markings on the outer panels of the vans indicated a volunteer group, and the transportation and equipment had all been donated.

Who would do this for nothing? At the time, I could not visualize how all human beings such be thought of as equal no matter what, and should be treated with respect and dignity. The body is merely a shell, a feeble host, and it is what's inside that really counts. The volunteers provide a great service and do this from their hearts. The handicapped are heroes making the best of what they have. I should have realized this, but never did.

Reality set in quickly, launched into the present once again, and my decision.

I could not make him stay. He obviously had some place to go. The oasis was surely not his home. I thought I better ask him of his intentions. He told me he must get back to the colony as soon as possible. I could not refuse him. He was a human being just like us and needed help.

After all, he had saved the old woman's life twice, once from the snake and the other from the poisoned water. He had proven to me he was not a threat. I know the old woman thought differently and did not want him along. I decided he would travel with us and we would take him back to his home.

Now I had the responsibility of two people. Two people that could look after themselves would be difficult enough, but these two posed a different set of complications. On top of that, they did not like each other. I was hoping last night's events would help the old woman build some trust. Time would tell. She still looked very uncomfortable and kept her distance. Two is company, and three's a crowd. I am sure that is exactly what she was thinking, or worse.

I announced we would travel together. The old woman turned away and started walking. I gave her a lengthy start, some space, than began to follow. The leper trudged along a fair distance from both of us. I presumed not to be unfriendly, but provide a suitable comfort zone for the old woman. A considerate move on his part I thought.

The path was no more, and I had to count on the old woman to lead the way. We marched through the desert in the comfort of the morning coolness. I thought I should speak to the old woman and try to convince her, the leper was our friend. She was walking a hundred feet away, so I began to jog over in her direction. I hoped I could talk some sense into her because I had no idea how long we would actually be together. Fighting and feuding would only make things more difficult. A little cooperation would go a long way in my books. I was hoping for the best, but expected any suggestion coming out of my little mouth would be given the cold shoulder.

Within hailing distance, I prepared by speech. I reached out, but was stopped in my tracks. Here we go again, the Voice had returned.

"RESPECT is a human condition spawning courtesy, politeness and etiquette, which distinguishes us from the animals. This is the conduct required to be a functional contributor to the family and society."

"RESPECT is a fundamental right of each individual. Dignity is a human condition of being worthy of respect or esteem. Respect is the objective, unbiased consideration and regard for the rights, values, beliefs, and property of all people. The concept of respect is commonly understood as "being civilized". The golden rule, do unto others as you would have them do unto you."

"RESPECT must be earned. You must give respect before you can get respect."

The Voice vapourized into nothingness as per usual, and I was left to ponder the complexities of what was happening. So many things to think about, to consider, to decide…truly mind boggling. I had to keep it together, I had to get home.

NINE

The Swamp

I CAUGHT UP WITH THE OLD WOMAN and tried to reason with her, but to no avail. She wasn't having any part of this. I could feel the pressure really starting to build, and even though the leper had saved her life I got the impression she was scared to death of him, and was not about to cut him any slack no matter what. I could only presume she believed getting too close would result in her contracting the disease, a simple touch may do the trick. I was not sure if that was true, just guessing. Could possibly be some other deep seeded reasons, maybe something personal and only privy to herself. I vowed to keep trying, but was not about to get my hopes up. She was stubborn for sure, but this seemed off the scales.

Lepers were a cursed lot, if you travel back in history. Many isolated locations were reserved for the lepers, to be on their own, to care for themselves, separated from society, scorned, and feared.

This method of detachment was procured to insure the lepers infliction did not spread. Tales of fingers, feet, and limbs falling off, resulted in most cultures and civilizations shunning these unfortunate invalids like the plague.

Out of sight, out of mind, no one wanted to see them or be associated with them. I now had sympathy for the lepers, their exile...their persecution. What could be going through his mind right now? He knew the old woman despised him and was probably thinking it was only a matter of time before the old woman corrupted my thinking, and turning me against him as well. I hope he wasn't thinking this. After what I had witnessed the leper do to prevent harm coming to the both of us, I was convinced, under all those bandages was a good heart.

I tried and tried, but the old woman would not bend, so I left her alone to her thoughts hoping she would come around. Up ahead, above the horizon, I began to see more tree tops and greenery. A tell tale sign our journey through the desert was about to end. Another hour and the desert gave way to thick foliage and forestation. The old woman pointed to an opening between the trees and we followed her. The footing here was different, soft and mushy, more like a marshy bog. The footing became quite treacherous, as with every step, my foot would sink an inch or two. I tried to locate some solid ground, so took the lead. The trek was incredibly slow and tense, trying to stay balanced and avoid the swarms of huge flies and gigantic mosquitoes. We passed small bubbling, gurgling pits of tar. Every burp sent foul smelling, possibly toxic vapours into the heavy air, suffocating our airways and contaminating our supply of oxygen.

I finally located some firmer soil and directed my companions to follow my exact steps. Our feet and legs were wet and muddy, the swamp difficult to navigate. I was always pushing branches and leaves out of my face so I could see where I was going. What a nuisance, what a headache. The old woman remained right behind me, with the leper about twenty metres behind her. I had the feeling she thought he was still too close, hoping he would get stuck, stranded, or just disappear into one of the boiling pits. We were in tight quarters here and had to stick together, careful at all times. We trudged along, the firm earth continued to be present, so we had to take advantage and make up for lost time. In the distance, I spotted something dangling from a small group of banyan trees. Peculiar from this vantage point,

I could not determine exactly what I was looking at.

The closer I came, the more gruesome the scene became. Heads...many small heads! I raised my arm, signaling the old woman to stop. I proceeded alone to check this out. Incredible...real heads, small, native looking, and scary. Could these truly be real? Further along I could see a structure that looked like a make shift alter. The area surrounding the stone structure was littered with skulls, bones, and stained in many shades of dark red. Maybe we had stumbled across some ceremonial area used for human sacrifice. The old woman had crept up behind me for a closer look, her curiosity getting the better of her. She gasped and grabbed her heart. I could hear the leper grown from further back. Both were obviously shocked at the revelations.

Swamps are legendary places brimming with tales of the occult, witches, cannibals, zombies, swamp monsters and the like. In books and movies, most swamps are haunted, considered places all fear to tread. Swamps rouse the imagination, trigger the senses, and are always draped in mystery.

With all this rolling around in my mind, I could only think of headhunters, and we unknowingly had just happened upon their trophy room. Witness to their handiwork, I could only hope we would not be next...frightening. I slowly began to scour the surroundings, alert to any sudden attack. Hundreds of cannibals could be watching from the jungle cover timing their ambush. My nerves were now in full swing, anticipating the worst. I was sure the old woman and the leper felt the same, terrified. Then out of no where, I heard an ear shattering SCREAM.

The cry for help came from up ahead, how far I could not determine, but it seemed to be straight ahead of us. I envisioned the headhunters finding another unsuspecting target. Momentarily frozen, I wondered if it best to stay here, or risk being captured. What was I going to do now? No help coming, I decided to investigate. Maybe not a sensible decision considering, but better than being caught here flatfooted, by a bunch of flesh eating savages. I hurried towards the sound, leaving my two companions behind. Again, the scream! I used the leper's blade to slash through the stringy vines and long leaves, finally arriving at the scene. A *Quickbog*!

I stopped quick as I had almost travelled to far. I was standing in front of a huge area of quicksand, and a young girl was struggling to keep her head above the surface. No headhunters in sight, I breathed a sigh of relief. The more the girl struggled and wiggled, the worse things got.

The old woman and the leper arrived to witness the girl's plight, staying a safe distance back, hidden amongst the dense foliage. I had to think quickly, the girl was sinking fast. I selected a long wispy branch and using the leper's blade to chop it off, now had a primitive device to attempt the rescue. I threw the branch out to the girl who was trashing about wildly, panicking and screaming. No good, just out of her reach. I circled the pit, trying to get closer. I knelt down and slid the branch along the top of the quicksand. She lunged forward and grabbed the end of the branch with one hand. I pulled it slowly and steadily towards me using both hands and all my strength. I stood and backed up using my legs for added power. She beginning to come to the top of the slurry. My plan was working to perfection when suddenly, a loud SNAP! The branch broke in half and the girl bolted backwards and began to sink once again.

Panic city, what now! I raced around the area looking for another suitable branch, but they all appeared too short. Scurrying around like a chicken with its head cut off, I was at a loss of what to do. In my haste, I was tripped up by a vine concealed beneath the grass. Like a trip rope game, I got caught, and feel flat on my face. I was stunned and angry. Looking down at my entangled foot, I noticed the vine, and instantly had an idea. I grabbed the vine and pulled. It ripped through the grass exposing its length. I kept pulling, then took my blade and chopped off piece about ten metres long. I tied a large knot at one end to give the cord some weight, and launched it softly out to the girl. Landing right beside her, she grabbed it and I began to pull with all y power. I pulled harder and faster until she was on the edge of the pit. I dropped the vine and ran to grab her arms, pulling her to safety.

She was covered in sandy slime, exhausted, and frightened. She lay prone on the ground gasping for air. Even covered with that ungodly sludge, she was incredibly beautiful. Her alabaster skin was like silk, highly unusual for a most probable indigenous type.

Her sand covered buckskin ensemble provided the clue. Raven coloured shoulder length hair, large innocent brown eyes, full lips, and the cutest little nose adorned her oval shaped face. This face I would never forget, mud or no mud, drop dead gorgeous. I had too much adrenalin pumping to feel the writhing pain in my aching muscles. The girl provided a welcomed distraction from the circumstances around me. I couldn't take my eyes off of her. What was she doing her? I hoped she would be alright. The old woman and the leper stood at a distance, separated, silently observing. As soon as the old woman noticed the leper too close, she began waving her arms frantically at him to get away, until she had created a comfortable space between them.

I assisted the young girl to a sitting position and try

to calm her, now that the ordeal was over and she was safe. Still out of breath, she began to come around, and looked at me, managing a half-hearted smile. I was out of breath as well and responded with a sheepish grin. I lowered my head, not wanting to give the impression I was staring at her. I did not want to make her feel uncomfortable. After all, she had just about died and now was in the company of three strangers. I hoped she was not afraid of us, and was not seriously injured.

I offered her a drink of coconut juice from my container. She hesitated then shyly accepted. Sipping slowly, I could see she cherished every drop. Several minutes later, the girl somewhat revived, was now able and willing to speak. She told me she had been on her way back to her village when something in the trees startled her. She thought it might be a panther, jaguar, or other big cat. She tripped, lost her balance, and fell into the quicksand. She panicked and thrashed about in the quickbog trying desperately to reach the edge, but only sank deeper. Trying to remain still did not work either, so she tried even harder and her situation worsened. Her only thought was to try and keep her head above the surface, survive as long as she could. She was about to go under when I arrived on the scene, a timely entrance you might say.

Without my chance appearance and instinctive action, she would have died. Taking a deep breath, she tried to stand. Her legs were still trembling causing her to bend over at the waist. Holding onto both legs with her hands for support, she straightened up, looked at the old woman and said nothing.

She spotted the leper and jumped back a few feet turning away. I reassured her he was not dangerous and related the story of how he had saved our lives. She did not seem convinced and did not want to look.

She turned to me and told me she was a tribal

princess, her father was the king. She was next in line to rule the village and was usually not allowed to venture off alone. She had sneaked away to try and enjoy some freedom, but now she knows why her father is always so protective. She learned a valuable lesson today and was lucky to be alive. I must have been sent by the gods she said. She told me she would give me a reward for saving her life and her village would treat me as a hero. A joyous celebration would ensue, including a feast I would never forget. I told her, no reward was necessary even though the offer sounded great. I sure could use a good meal. She kept insisting, but I kept noticing the word "me". I seemed to be the only one included in the festivities, and that assumption was soon confirmed.

She offered to take me to her village and then I would be escorted by her tribe to where I needed to go. She only made this offer to me, not the old lady or the leper. I asked if I could bring them, and she was defiant, a definite no.

I asked why and she replied. She told me the old woman was not from her tribe, maybe an enemy, maybe a witch. Her tribe would abandon her in the swamp to die or worse, as they did not like outsiders, considering them bad luck. The leper would be put to death immediately because her tribe feared his condition. She did not want to be responsible for what may happen to them. I on the other hand, was a different story. I saved her life, and in her eyes, the others did nothing to help, so she could offer them nothing. She suggested I leave them in the swamp to find their way since they said they knew where they were going. That may be true, but the swamp was a dangerous place for me to just leave them to fend for themselves. She offered no assistance to them at all, but maintained I would find the way much quicker with her tribe's help. She could guarantee my safety through the swamp and would be led to path I needed to follow.

The offer was extremely tempting I had to admit, but leaving the old woman and the leper at the mercy of the swamp was to me, unthinkable and cold blooded. I could not do it.

I explained my position, my reasoning, but she seemed puzzled as to why these people were so important to me. They were strangers, not friends, not family, expendable, just leave them and save yourself. She said I should be selfish and live. The practicality made sense but the reality did not, not to me anyway. I could not leave these two people out here alone, never knowing whether they survived or not. I could not live with this on my mind for the rest of my life. I just could not.

The princess shook her head as I politely refused her offer time and time again. She repeated the offer one final time, but I gave her the same answer. She conceded and said she would guide us through part of the swamp and then would head off in the direction of her village. Better than nothing. I offered her some figs and she ate slowly and drank more juice. After a little nourishment, she seemed steadier on her feet and was ready to go. The princess took the lead, as she knew the trail. We followed for about thirty minutes and then she stopped. She pointed straight ahead. She was taking another route, even though I couldn't clearly see one. Before departing, the princess opened a pouch she had dangling around her neck. She removed a flat, round object. Resembling a coin, it seemed to be made of jade, about the size of a silver dollar, with a thin band of pure gold running through it.

She presented it to me as a token of her gratitude. I did not want to accept. I deserved nothing for doing what anyone else would have done. She declared it would be a great insult to her, her tribe, and the king, if I did not accept. Since she put it that way, I reluctantly but happily accepted.

She also had a warning for us. We must be careful, to beware the tree with the "seeing eye". I really could not comprehend what she was talking about, but I hoped I would recognize it when I saw it. I turned to see if the old woman and the leper were close at hand and not strangling each other. As expected, I found them far apart, eating the figs and paying no attention to me or each other. I turned back, the princess was GONE!

Impossible, where did she go? There did not seem to be another path. See just vanished. I stood there puzzled and quite taken by surprise. I did not want to see her go, at least not like that. She was beautiful, enchanting, and mysterious, so I had hoped to wave a proper good-bye, like something you read about in fairy tales. The princess was Snow White, Sleeping Beauty, and Cinderella all rolled into one. Now she was gone, gone forever I would suspect. She made me feel good, alive, and energized. I would lock her image in my mind and use it for inspiration. Good idea.

I felt a bit special right now, but was reminded of my sporting days at school. I could clearly recollect many occasions where my loyalty waned, or was absolutely non existent. In school I was a superior athlete, the best. Even though I was not large in stature, I was very quick, fast, coordinated, and athletically intelligent. I was a highly sought after commodity on the playing field at school and around the neighbourhood. An athlete extraordinaire, I ruled the playing field, proud of my talents and abilities.

Whatever side I played with usually won, and everyone liked to win. On many occasions, I would abandon my usual group of friends who were inferior athletes, and join the group of larger, stronger, more athletic types when it came to school yard competitions. This way I was pretty much guaranteed a winning result, and that made me feel good. I really didn't care how my so called real friends" thought about it. They lost, I won, that's all that really matters. I always said, "It's not whether you win or lose, it's everything."

I used to shed friends like water off a duck's back. What is a real friend anyway. They come and go, probably hundreds during your school life, so who needs them, really. I never imagined a human being would be lucky to have one or two good friends during a lifetime, and need them too. I had no idea what being a good friend meant. I certainly was not a good friend to anyone, and never lost any sleep over it. The most important person in the world was me.

I came out of my stupor and walked over to my fellow travellers. I questioned them about the sudden disappearance of the princess, and asked if they had seen where the she had gone. They had not and were totally disinterested.

I thought it wise to share the story about the "seeing eye" tree, hoping one of them would have some knowledge of it, but they had no response. I motioned it was time to go, as I now knew the way. They rose to their feet and the three of us were off again.

It was slow motion through the steamy swamp, the ankle high methane fog blanketing the soft footing. I slashed the branches away, continuously creating a larger opening for our advance. The bugs, mostly mosquitoes, were intensely irritating and annoying. I was hoping no big cats like the ones the princess mentioned were lurking in the treetops waiting to pounce. I glanced upwards on many occasions but found nothing peculiar. I instructed my fellow travellers to be on alert and be careful since they were behind me and I must concentrate on what is ahead of us.

The trail became wider and the earth firmer. We came upon a clearing with one very unique tree in the centre. Like a group of Banyan tress intertwined, this swamp monarch stood guarding the entrance to a tunnel of trees. This looked like a great place for a picnic, so decided all should rest for a few minutes. I took a seat on a nearby stump and the old woman walked up to the massive Banyan tree. She began touching it, examining, apparently reading the writing on the wall of bark. The trunk was massive. I had never seen anything like it. Possibly someone had carved their initials on the tree or there was some interesting graffiti or artwork there. She seemed enthralled and soon the leper was getting drawn into the mystique. I watched from a distance. After all, it was just a tree. The leper tried to view from a distance off to the side of the old woman. She was up close and personal, nose right against the gritty skin. I thought this to be amusing and harmless fun, so I let them at it, I needed rest.

I closed my eyes, tired from the morning's harrowing adventure. I started to doze off and began dreaming. In my dream I saw the tree, the old woman, and the leper. What were they doing in my dream? I wanted a different one. Bring back the princess, please. Something was wrong, disturbing...unreal. The dream was quickly turning into a nightmare. Loud creaks and cracks woke me from my slumber. Through my sleepy eyes I witnessed the unimaginable.

The old woman and the leper had been captured by the limbs of the Banyan tree. Like a giant octopus, the trees had them tied up and was flailing them about in the air. I jumped to my feet, blinking and rubbing my eyes, startled at what I saw. What the...this can't be real? This must be the tree the tribal princess was talking about. Could our timing be any worse? How could we know this was the tree we were supposed to avoid. Looked like any other big old tree. Suddenly, I remembered seeing some picture in a book some time ago, a mythical man eating tree called the *Madagascar tree*. Not sure this was one and the same, but I did not have the luxury of time to figure this out. My companions were in deep trouble and I had to rescue them. No phone booth in site to change into some superhero with super powers, just me against the tree. I knew there would be days like this...not really!

The tree was hoisting them about, playing with them, like rag dolls. The princess said this tree had a seeing eye, but where, no evidence of that. I had to take her word, her tribe must know. I ran into the trees to look for a suitable spear. I located one about two metres long, took out the blade, and quickly sharpened one end. I ran back near the tree and poised the make shift javelin for a strike. Hitting the bark would achieve nothing. I had to observe closely and then make my move. I watched and watched as my two companions were being terrorized. The leper's bandages were starting to unravel and he was moaning in pain. The old woman was screaming for the attack to stop. Could this tree really eat people? Not sure, and I wasn't about to wait and find out. At the very least, the tree could cause enough traumas to kill these two weak and helpless individuals.

I had to be nimble to avoid being snatched up by the other predatory tentacles. I danced from side to side, back and forth, out of reach, but had to get closer for a clear shot. The branches were continuously after me as well. The tree seemed determined to capture me, enticing me closer, using my friends as bait. I bobbed and weaved, jumped forward then back trying to get closer. This strategy was too risky, and I had nothing to shoot at, really didn't know what to look for. The game of cat and mouse continued. I knew I would recognize the opportunity when I saw it. Suddenly, there it was.

A slit in the tree bark exposed what looked like an eye. I guess the tree was trying to size me up, risking a revealing look. This was the chance I had been hoping for. I stepped in closer, dodging the branches and took dead aim from five metres out. Hurling the harpoon with all my might, I watched the wooden lance find its mark.

"BANG!"

I scored a direct hit, right in the eye. The branches holding my compatriots released them immediately. The tree squealed with pain, and all the   branches began flapping away wildly in the air. With the tree distracted and in great pain, I gathered up the old woman and the leper and lead them out of reach.

The tree limbs continued to thrash uncontrollably and finally they stopped. The mighty Banyan let out on final deafening squeal, than the entire tree drooped and began to disintegrate before our very eyes. I had slain the mighty dragon. Soon there was nothing except a large rotted tree stump…a tombstone for the "seeing eye" tree. It was over and everyone was safe.

I checked them both for injuries and there appeared to be nothing of a serious nature. They were both shaken up, literally, and still afraid. The old woman could not stop trembling and the leper was quivering. I showed them what was left of the tree, nothing, and this seemed to have a soothing effect. This tree would never take anyone again, it was gone. We rested for a hour or so, regained our composure, and thought it best to try and find our way out of the swamp.

A chirping sound caught my attention, and I searched the tree tops. Once again, I spotted my little friend the blue jay. He must have witnessed the entire event from a safe vantage point and now was here to lend support. He stretched his wings and flew off out of sight through the trees.

The princess had warned us, and without knowing about the eye, the old woman and leper would have been killed. There was no way I could have accepted the princess' offer and leave these two to fend for themselves. We came here together, and we will leave here together. I motioned for them to get on their feet and press on, so we did. A few minutes later, you guessed it, the Voice.

"LOYALTY is a faithfulness and allegiance to master and cause. Your words and actions are one, no promises necessary. Loyalty is sometimes built on personal bonds of mutual obligation"

"LOYALTY is a virtue that supports all success and we must also be loyal to our own goals, plans, objectives and the realistic path of attainment. Being honest with ourselves is imperative in defining such a realistic path."

"LOYALTY duty to family, expressed as filial piety, is a fundamental aspect of this virtue.

The voice dissipated, gone once again, without a trace, and of course, no help offered. What could be next? What could be waiting for us just around the corner? By now, I must have seen it all...or maybe not.

TEN

The Valley

AN EMINENT DISASTER AVERTED, I led the way, guiding the three of us along the extension of the trail the princess had instructed me to follow. We battled our way through the dense foliage being ever aware the danger hiding amongst the shadows. Luckily, we did not experience any further perilous encounters. Maybe I spoke to soon. A loud howling screech echoed through the treetops. The sudden audible assault silenced the jungle and stopped us dead in our tracks. I instinctively surveyed the area. The old woman was down on one knee, her bulky dress pulled over her head providing a form of camouflage. The leper had crossed arms covering his face. None of us knew what to expect.

The roar from the big cat made the hairs on the back of my neck stand up. The princess had mentioned jaguars and panthers, so they must be native to this habitat. Scary...very scary! I only had the blade for protection, but let's face it, the three us would be easy prey for these skilled killers of the rainforest. I searched for signs of moving branches, an indicator we were being hunted. No way to counteract the cat's keen sense of smell and stealth approach, we could only wait in silence, and pray the danger would pass. After fifteen minutes or so, I presumed the predator had found a tastier meal, so I motioned to my companions it was time to move on. We had to find the exit immediately, before one of the other jungle beasts decided it was dinner time.

Being quick afoot was not really an option for our troupe, but I have to admit, I had never seen those two move this fast before. We picked up the pace and within thirty minutes, the vegetation thinned, and we soon came to the end of the jungle swamp. What a relief. I pushed aside the final few branches and before us, a lush, unpretentious, far-reaching valley. I stood in awe of this miraculous transition, a sight to behold, but a most welcome one.

The old woman pointed far into the distance and told me she lived on one side of this valley, and the leper said he lived on the opposite side, along the outskirts of this same valley. A strange coincidence perhaps, but good news from a logistical point of view. The only question...how large was this valley? On second thought, the logistics created yet another set of unwelcome circumstances. Decisions...decisions, here I go again...great. Whose village should we go to first? How widespread exactly was this valley? The old woman was far off to the side and offered no assistance. Obviously she was thinking of being reunited with her family as soon as possible. I'm certain she anticipated we would go to her village first. I truly wanted to grant her wish, and would have, but not so simple. Standing there, I began to think, and came up with what thought a logical solution. Without saying exactly why, I told them we would take the leper home first. I truly believed the leper needed to return to his colony as soon as possible. He needed to be where he could access assistance and medicine or medical supplies. I never asked, but it was possible he was bringing such supplies back to the colony and his compatriots required his immediate return.

I considered several other reasons as well, and upon hearing my announcement, the old woman became visibly upset, she wanted to go home first. I really couldn't blame her, I would feel the same. I could not just leave her to make it home alone, so I guided her off to the side and tried to explain. I had the feeling, no matter whatever I said, was not going to convince or comfort her, so I spared the small talk and cut to the chase.

If we took her home first, the people in her village would panic at the sight of the leper and they may harm him or even worse. I was concerned for everyone's welfare and could not chance anyone getting hurt so close to the homecoming. There was no love lost between her and the leper, and she had no problem making it obvious. Now she felt like she had lost and he had won. Of course, this was not the case, but in her eyes that's exactly what happened. I know she was angry with me, but I honestly believed the decision was correct. Having no real choice, she reluctantly agreed to accompany us to the leper's colony.

I understood she was old and needed to get home, yet I had to decide what I thought best for all. Decisions, decisions…so difficult…why? I had never had to make any before. They were all made for me, the important ones anyways. I never gave it a thought until now. I was guessing there would be more to come. I would deal with them one at a time.

I agreed to make sure she got home safely, so no other explanations were necessary, promising we would get there by tomorrow evening at the latest. Night fall was approaching, so we would camp at this end of the valley tonight and deliver everyone home tomorrow. I was hopeful this included me. The old woman continued to display her disapproval. She marched off in a huff and settled down for the night, a measurable distance from both of us. Guess she decided to exile both of us for the time being.

We were early risers once again, getting used to it as a matter of fact. Sleep did not seem so necessary today of all days, as we were all anxious to get started. We set off over the rolling hills and down into the valley.

There was nothing for as far my eyes could see, just valley. By mid afternoon we were still pushing forward, content with our pace, seemingly in the middle of nowhere, been there a lot lately. The leper and the old woman knew they would be home soon. I was the only one not so certain. The leper had us follow his lethargic lead through the hills and tall grass until finally, far off in the distance, I noted a very distinctive depression, bordered by a semi circular wall of white stone. We all stopped.

The face of this stone wall appeared to have been a sheared off hillside, exposing the rocky interior. The cliff face was dotted with hundreds of holes. We were a long way off, so I really could not get a proper perspective. The leper pointed towards the rock face. This must be it, home, the leper colony, dead ahead.

We marched on steadily and now within several hundred metres revealing what could have been an old quarry, possibly limestone. The entire area was situated in a shallow recess, and the holes were actually caves in the cliffs. This quarry must have been abandon for many years, maybe hundreds of years, until the exiled lepers adopted this formidable landscape as their new home. Lepers are sensitive to light, so prefer a darker environment. Long rope ladders adorned each entrance, but there was no sign of life. We kept moving forward until the leper signaled us to stop.

Everything was quiet, too quiet. Where was everyone? Surely his family would come to greet him. No response, what was going on? I looked back at the old woman who was staring daggers at the leper. I could only guess, for whatever reason, she assumed the leper was up to something...something no good. I had no idea what was about to happen next. I only knew something was about to happen, I could take that to the bank. Looking back at the leper, he began to fiddle with his clothing.

The leper reached inside his weather worn bandages and pulled out a small bone of some sort. He put it up to his lips and blew. What the bone produced was a sharp, piercing, high pitched sound, which caused me to cover my ears. He stopped, than blew again. Twice was enough. Movement could not be detected. From out of the darkness of the caves came hordes of lepers.

They congregated in the mouths of the caves and waited. The leper gave them one more ear piercing burst and then the entire colony began climbing down the ladders. Hundreds and hundreds, a proverbial beehive, incredible! The throngs had now reached the ground and began limping, crawling, and dragging themselves in our direction.

I looked back at the old woman who immediately turned and began striding quickly away. What was she doing? Where was she going in such a rush? No patience I guess. Maybe she just thought it was her turn now and wanted to get a head start. Not very polite, but understandable. I was quite certain the lepers were coming to thank us, so turned toward them and smiled. The crowd began to make noise, ugly guttural sounds, not the most welcoming tune. The lepers were advancing like an army. I noticed most of them carrying staffs, knives, and axes...a real attention getter. What for? The leper turned to me, thanked me, and suggested I leave as soon as possible. He explained, outsiders would come here to kill the lepers, so all were not welcome. If the lepers caught any outsiders, they would allegedly torture, kill, and eat them, although he mentioned he had never witnessed such an event. He told me it might be a good idea to leave now as a precaution. In fact, run would be a better precaution...NOW!

I accepted his advice and bolted off. The old woman was a quarter mile ahead of me, but I would be there soon. I could still hear the growling, so I just kept on running. I glanced back over my shoulder a few times to see the advancing hordes stop and surround their comrade. They all started making their way back to the safety of the colony. I thought I saw the leper glance in our direction, but I could not be sure.

I quickened my pace in an effort to catch up to the old woman. She was still motoring along at high speed, high speed for her anyways, and had put some distance between us. One last glance back toward the colony, then I stopped and turned around. I must have been a half mile away, and could see little or no evidence of the pitted rock face. The walls of the quarry seemed unscathed and the lepers were nowhere to be seen.

I should not have been surprised considering what I had witnessed up to this point, but I was. Where did they go? Were they ever there? Was the leper real? Wow...incredible! I turned my attention to the old woman up ahead. Within a few minutes I had caught up with her. She scolded me repeatedly for making her go to the colony. I knew she was real! I felt bad, but I still think it was the correct decision considering the circumstances. Now it was her turn to take me to the other side of the valley, and her home, if she didn't kill me first. I felt a great sense of relief having returned the leper to his home and now the second half of my commitment was about to be fulfilled. I was sure this part would be simpler, uncomplicated, and satisfying. That's what I kept telling myself...I'm such a liar. The duties and obligations to my fellow travellers would soon be fait de complete, and I could finally concentrate on me finding my way home.

The valley rolled along methodically, but the way was clear now, no chance of getting lost or side tracked.

I was actually looking forward to this. Finally meeting some real people with friendly faces would be a welcome relief. At least that is what I thought. I plodded along staying within shouting distance, giving the old woman some space. I thought she would show more expression being so close to home, but she just stared straight ahead, never glancing in my direction. Suddenly everything around us became quiet, real quiet...too quiet. The old woman stopped and slowly looked over her shoulder. I followed her line of sight and saw the reason for her concern.

A large black funnel was forming on the horizon, increasing in size every second. The old woman looked at me and started to run. Her weak limbs could not muster much speed and I jogged along beside her. I began to run backwards, keeping an eye on our pursuer. The tornado was gathering speed and was now some twenty stories high. We had no obvious escape route. Directly on its line, we could now feel the power of this giant centrifuge. Running backwards, I soon whizzed past the old woman who for some unknown reason decided to stop. She stomped on the ground again and again. The twister was advancing quickly and the wind was making it difficult for me to hustle over to the old woman. I had to get to her.

Suddenly, she knelt down, grabbed onto something in the grass, and pulled. A trapdoor opened exposing a hidden shelter beneath the earth.

She climbed down the ladder into the hole and I was right behind her. I closed the trap door using the strap handle, and stared at the old woman. How did she know about this place? This must have happened before. People from her village must have built the bunker, maybe several of them, and lucky for us they did. The tornado rumbled overhead, dislodging dirt from the interior walls, and spraying us with it. We covered our faces, crouched down, and lowered our heads.

The sound of the mighty funnel cloud gyrating overhead was deafening. The trapdoor began rattling violently, so I grabbed the leather strap and held on with all my strength. We endured ten minutes of pure sensory torture, than finally the enemy gave up. I cautiously lifted the trap door, stealing a peek, trying to spot the funnel, but not a trace in sight. I assisted the old woman out of the subterranean pothole, and we brushed the dirt off of our clothes, face, and hair. I shook my head in disbelief. We were so close, and yet, in the wink of an eye it could have been all for nothing, finished, sucked up into space and flung across galaxy. Lucky to be alive, I was thankful.

The old woman wasted little time, reestablished her bearings, and marched on in earnest. At this juncture, I was her willing sidekick, constantly on the watch for further unwelcome anomalies. The trek took many hours, but nearing dusk I could see something on the horizon, a settlement. The old woman pointed and acknowledged this was her village. She was fatigued, but subtlety excited to see her home. I was hoping these villagers would not chase me out like the lepers, but I had to wait and see. As we approached, with no red carpet or welcome mat on offer, I was anxious and nervous. Closer and closer, I began to perspire, not feeling the love you might say.

A hundred metres out, villagers started gathering, and a few headed in our direction. I am sure they recognized the old woman, but probably wondered who I was and what I was doing with one of their citizens. A handful of settlers came to greet us. It became obvious from the smiles, that most of these people were members of her immediate family. They hugged and kissed her and two other women began to weep, her

117

daughters I was told. The villagers shook my hand and told me, she had wandered off a few weeks ago and could not be located. They feared she was dead and it was nothing short of a miracle to see her alive again. All were joyous, and everyone in the village was ecstatic.

The return of the old woman was great cause for celebration and a feast was to be organized in her honour. Who was this woman? Why was she so important? I learned during the walk back to the village, the old woman was a bit of a soothsayer, and could correctly predict the weather, therefore improving their chances of a good harvest.

Without that, the village could not survive, they needed her talents. An interesting story, but the feast was what I was waiting for. The locals were cooking up a storm and the aromas were amazing, with all kinds of meats, chicken, beef, lamb, you name it. Truly a feast fit for a king.

This was the biggest buffet I had ever seen, the tables measuring thirty metres in length. The entire village was there to celebrate. What a great occasion. The old woman was seated at the head of the table and I beside her. The feast was on. I ate slowly, sampling everything I could and trying to make small talk with the villagers. This was really fun and I was hoping I was at the end of my journey. As I continued to eat, I observed everyone enjoying the occasion, asking the old woman a thousand questions, but not one person mentioned anything about my plight. Tummy on overload, I reluctantly had to give in, enough. Everyone was pretty much finished, and started leaving the table, taking turns thanking me for helping the old woman return safely.

After dinner, I was given a tour of the small village which was spread out and sandwiched between two beautiful streams. The setting was tranquil and serene. I was left alone to wander about, and found a cozy spot beneath a weeping willow tree. I sat silently listening to the stream's calming rhapsody. What a peaceful setting. I began to reflect about family and what family really means, why family is so important.

All these years I had never really thought about all the things my parents do or have done for me. I thought taking care of me was their duty, their job, their responsibility. How tough could it be? I am so easy to care fore, such a great kid. I never thought of ever looking after or having to care for my parents. They can look after themselves, right? Even if they get old, they have each other to handle things, why would I have to do anything? Why should I be responsible for their welfare, kids don't look after parents, it is the other way around I always thought.

When my mom got sick I did not have to do anything, dad did it. I don't even remember asking my mom how she felt, just went about my business, school, playing outside, pretend I was studying, the usual. Grandparents...what about them?

They are always nice to me because I don't see them that often. I don't think my parents look after them, but I remember my parents helping them do lots of things around their home. I never really realized how people look after each other, especially families until I came to this village. They all seem to care for each other, help each other, and get along with each other. I guess families are supposed to do that, look out for each other. Maybe my parents do more for me than I think? Right now I have to figure out how to find my way home so I can find them. So many unanswered questions and right now I feel there is no end in sight. After all the elation...a serious let down. Was this journey ever going to end? Parish the thought, I would rather die first, and that may happen yet.

Was I any further ahead then I was a few days ago? How could I know? Was the end here or near? Didn't seem like it. Where were all these keys? Would I find them at the end of my journey or was I still at the beginning? I really had no way of gauging anything and this was very unsettling. I was hoping these people would show me the way or take me home, this must be the end. I waited for an answer, hoping someone would come up to me and tell me, no such luck, no one came.

All through dinner, not a soul, not even the old woman, had mentioned a thing about my home, so I was assuming I had somewhere else to go or to get to. As much as I was looking forward to tomorrow, I was very apprehensive. I had been through so much and still no end in sight. I told myself to knock it off and just deal with it. That is all I could do. If there is more, than so be it.

I was about to leave when I heard the sound of a solitary song bird. I smiled and did not even have to guess, the blue jay. There it was in all its splendor, chirping a cheerful tune. I was not sure what he was so happy about, must have had a better day than me. I waved good-bye, stood up, and strolled back to the old woman's home. Exhaustion was starting to set in quickly, totally worn out.

I was given facilities to shower and a comfortable bed to sleep in. What a treat. I never appreciated things like these before, always taking them for granted. I planned to have the best sleep of my life. Tomorrow was a new day. I lay my head down and closed my eyes. I was about to doze off when I heard it, the Voice.

"FILIAL PIETY is the love and respect for one's parents, coupled with the willingness to care for them without compromise or condition."

"FILIAL PIETY may also include respect for the

family lineage, grand parents and ancestors."

Confucius was most probably the first, and most profound proponent of FILIAL PIETY. His philosophy decried this virtuous concept be deeply entrenched in the Chinese culture.

Honour thy father and thy mother.

I heard the Voice fade away. I had nothing to add, so I faded out with it.

ELEVEN

The Mountain

I WAS UP AT THE BREAK OF DAWN, the usual for me these days. I wasn't alone, the entire village seemed to be operating at full speed. I peered out my window while dressing and saw many familiar faces from the night before, bustling about their daily routines. I made my way down the wooden staircase sniffing the air. The aroma of bacon frying and coffee brewing was a welcome change from the past few days. I strolled into the kitchen and was greeted by the old woman and her daughter. They were preparing breakfast for the household. A few minutes later the entire family gathered in the kitchen, all taking their seats. They treated me like part of the family and I felt very comfortable. Again the family expressed their gratitude for what I had done and promised to care for their parents with love and compassion.

Breakfast over, I began to say my good-byes. The family had prepared a backpack for me, with rope, tools, all kinds of things they said I would need. They also stuffed as much food as they could into the pack without crushing it. The backpack was fairly heavy, but I was not complaining, I was sure every single item would come in handy. The old woman looked me, and placed her hand gently on my shoulder. Her sons said they would take me as far as they could and show me the way I must travel. The four of us set off.

I could see a huge mountain directly ahead and the sons told me I must follow the mountain road. My escorts explained, the mountain was dangerous, treacherous, and no one from the village would dare to travel there. The mountain was volcanic and prone to violent eruptions, not to mention horrific weather patterns, wild animals, and possibly some bandits or thieves.

Now I was beginning to worry. I wish they hadn't told me anything. I was really apprehensive, thinking I may not be able to make it on my own. My confidence was dwindling. The sons kept telling me things I should do, not do, watch for, the usual. Then they related one little known fact about the mountain. Not one person who went up the mountain had ever returned. Just great! I really didn't need to hear that. What was I doing? Sounds like suicide. If no adult had ever returned, what were my chances. I was thinking zero. Apparently the path I must follow was on this mountain. I kept thinking, though no one had ever returned from the village, I was not returning, I was going. Returning...going...there is a difference right? Not sure, but I'll keep telling myself there is. I'll tell myself just about anything if it will help preserve my sanity.

We finally reached the base of the mountain and I stood silently staring at a sheer cliff face. A rope ladder hung from the top of the escarpment. I must first climb the ladder, seventy metres or so, than I would reach the plateau. A four hundred metre walk and then the real climb would begin. I shook their hands and told them how much I appreciated their hospitality and friendship. I waved my final good-bye and began to climb the ladder. A few metres up I looked back and everyone was gone, not a trace. I should have been able to see them from up here, but all I saw was the valley grass waving the tree leaves rustling. Puzzling, not so unexpected, I was all alone once more, just me against the mountain, not a fair fight, advantage mountain.

As I climbed the ladder I suddenly remembered the "keys". I hadn't received any or found any. I was supposed to have ten and I did not even have one. Where were they? Maybe I would get them all in one shot? I hoped the keys would sort themselves out because I had to focus on getting to the top of this mountain, why was still a mystery. I struggled the final few metres, hoisting myself onto the plateau. I could now see the full majesty of the snow-capped mountain.

I was hoping I really did not have to get to the top because I would certainly freeze to death. I had no clothes for ice and snow. I strode bravely onward, my greatest obstacle staring me in the face. Soon I was standing in awe, a narrow path directly in front of me. It was the only one, no guessing games here. I was as ready as I'll ever be, so took a deep breath and began my mountain assault.

The pathway through the lower mountain forest was rocky, but the incline was gradual and not too strenuous. The tall trees blocked out most of the sun, so the path was dimly lit at best. The elevation had already effected the temperature and it was much cooler than in the village. They had packed me a sweater, so I stopped and put it on. One less thing to carry I thought. The area seemed pretty quiet, only the sounds of a few birds in the treetops and the odd creak and crack...nothing too serious. Every hour or so I would stop and rest, drink some water, and nibble at some fruit or piece of chicken. This was kind of like a picnic in the park, just a lonely one. Everything was fine until I heard a loud roar. The sound was definitely not the roar from the motor of a muscle car. This sounded like a bear, a very large bear.

I would definitely recognize the sound of a mountain lion or wolf, so through the process of elimination I determined it must be a bear. How close and how large, I could not tell, only imagine. It really did not matter because any size bear was too big in my books. I stood still, hoping not to draw attention, but I knew the bear may have already smelled me since they can smell for miles. I was hoping I was upwind and my scent would be much less detectable. Difficult to tell amongst the trees, I could only hope. Just in case, I tried to recall what to do. According to television documentaries, I should play dead if attacked. That wouldn't be too difficult, because I would be dead. I was doing a good job scaring myself, so decided to lay on the ground, keep my scent out of the wind. I closed my eyes and heard another loud bellow. Not sure if this one was closer or farther, didn't mater, the animal was still too close for comfort.

Many minutes passed and I heard no further indications the creature was near, so I picked myself up and continued up the mountain path. Late in the afternoon the terrain began to change, more rock and the path was steeper, making the climb more demanding. A squirrel startled me as it darted across the track. I smiled, pretty jumpy now. Better the squirrel than the bear.

The path was leading towards the edge of the mountain and narrowed considerably. Soon I was looking at the side of the mountain, a two hundred metre drop to the base and only a path a foot wide to stand on. I must be in the wrong place, this could not be. The path was gone. The path was now more like a balance beam and I was not a gymnast. I moved my backpack around front and placed my back against the cliff face. I walked sideways trying not to look down, not even straight ahead. I looked to my left side only, noting the direction of the footpath as it curved around the side of the mountain. The curve was a sweeping one and I was unable to guess how long I would have to balance myself walking sideways. One wrong step and it would be all over.

Carefully and cautiously, I moved in tune with the curvature. I heard rocks beginning to tumble down the side of the mountain. Loose impediment from above was now bouncing off my head. The rocks became larger and sailed passed me down cliff face. Many smaller stones were collecting on the pathway making the footing a problem. I feared the worst, an all out rock slide. I had no cover, no protection, so if this was the case, I was doomed.

The base was now covered in gravel and not solid. I had to slide my feet through the particles, but this snow plow effect was causing a worse pile up as I moved along. Some huge boulders bounded down the mountainside and I was truly frightened. Another huge rock just missed my head so I stopped and waited. I wasn't sure if I should move or not. Probably wiser just to wait it out. The rocks kept coming in decreasing increments, a good sign. I stood fast, my back flat against the rocky face. A few minutes later, the rumbling stopped with only a pebble or two bounding downwards. I carefully continued around the corner and finally saw the path widen back onto the main trail. I was relieved to see freedom only a few metres away, but had to take a breather, the walkway was still very narrow and dangerous. I proceeded ever so cautiously, making sure the final few steps were not my last. I plowed along finally reaching the end of the terrifying trail.

Now back on the mountain roadway, I felt more at ease. I marched on and soon came across an area surrounded by glaciers. They seemed to be concealing a giant crater, probably millions of years old. I walked down onto the glaciers and slid along like an amateur ice skater. It was fun, but I was too tired to enjoy it. I had to cross the glacier to meet the roadway up ahead. Slippery and tiring, this was no easy trek. I clumsily glided across the slick surface when suddenly I heard a faint cracking sound...then a louder one. I skidded to a halt and looked behind me. The ice was cracking, and cracking fast. Not sure if I was on top of a crater lake or not, but sure didn't want to find out. I put it back in high gear, glancing behind every few seconds. Water was gushing out as the ice split, separating into huge chunks. This was not good. I was about to be turned into a giant popsicle. Maybe this is where everyone else who ventured here had met their demise? I found running backwards allowed me more traction, and I could keep an eye on the breaking ice.

I was moving quite quickly now, but the ice was parting faster as well, if fact, like a freight train without brakes. Closer and closer, the sound of cracking ice became deafening. Now within only a few metres of me, I was scared to death. Only a few metres away, the back of my ankles struck something and I went flying. Hitting a small slope, I rolled down a gentle incline as the ice crashed against the bank. I was safe. I stood up and observe the massive pieces of ice floating atop the lake. I let out a sigh of relief, my heart still pounding.

Now on the other side of the ice field, I noticed the path heading straight up. The climb was going to get tough. I thought to take it slow and conserve energy. Still lots of daylight remaining, so no urgency at this moment to over exert myself. I still had my hickory walking stick for support, and was on my way. What a hike this was going to be. I hated hiking, but that is all I had been doing for the past few days. Once this is over, if this ever ends, I promised myself I would never hike again.

Several hours passed, and the uphill excursion was taking its toll. The path emerged from the thinning forestation into a large rocky clearing. The appearance unique, these rocks were not just rocks. They looked like ruins of some sort. All the stones seemed strategically placed, not randomly scattered. This could have been an ancient settlement many hundreds or even thousands of years ago. I decided to stay here the night and tackle the colder elevation in the morning when the sun came up. The air was nippy and the wind was swirling. Darkness...cold...mountain, better play it safe. I would stay here for the night.

With a couple hours of light left, I decided to explore the area. Ancient history is my favourite subject. I would pretend to be an explorer and to try to determine who may have been here, the Romans, Celts, native Americans, or possibly some unknown civilization. This was really exciting. The area was large enough to be a small city. Climbing higher I noticed something, a graveyard. The graves were marked with stones and strangely constructed crosses, the black sticks arranged in an unusual geometric pattern. The cemetery was definitely centuries old. I bet many a secret lay buried beneath the sod. The tombstones, triangular shape, resembled mini pyramids. Various inspirations adorned the edifice; however the text was not familiar. I needed a real expert to solve this puzzle. Who could they belong to? I remember the old woman's sons saying no one had ever returned from the mountain. Maybe they lay here, but what could have happened? How...why?

My findings were fascinating and I was pumped up. I wanted to stay here and really investigate. Darkness came too soon and I took my place a ways from the graveyard, amongst the scattered fortifications. I lay down and looked up at the stars. I spotted the little dipper, and began to count. Worked better than counting sheep! I faded off into dreamland.

Maybe two hours had passed when I suddenly I awoke to a strange sound. It was not the Voice. A muffled "huffing" sound could be clearly heard. I jumped to my feet and strained my eyes in the darkness. I saw nothing. Then I heard more sounds, like the shouting of warriors as they charged to engage the enemy. I heard the pounding hooves of horses as they thundered passed me towards the grave site. White stringy clouds dashed past me. What was going on? I felt I was in the middle of a war, but there were no soldiers, or at least none I could see.

Then the white flashes were everywhere, dancing to the sounds of the battle. I bobbed and weaved to avoid being hit, but soon there was too many and they seemed to pass right through me. The sound of armies clashing in battle was unmistakable. Armaments against shields, yelling and screaming, wounded steeds falling to the ground, the chaos most horrid…terror all around. I could envision the combat, yet I could see absolutely nothing apart from the white wisps whizzing frantically in all directions. The onslaught continued. This was like the reverse of a silent film, only now there was sound but no picture. I ran towards the graveyard and watched from a distance. The blizzard of white intensified, like a feeding frenzy amongst hungry sharks. I heard a horn blare, and he wisps of white vanished, and the sounds died. The battle was over.

What had I just witnessed? A war between two legions of ghosts? I should be scared to death, but instead, wanted to see more. Who were these warriors, these brave souls, and what happened here. No sleep tonight, not a chance. I would stay awake and wait for part two. Hour after hour, I stayed poised for more action but received nothing of the kind, it was really over. I was disappointed, but at the same time lucky to have been a witness to the event. I had always wanted to meet a real ghost, maybe I just did. This had been exhilarating and terrifying at the same time, how weird.

129

I thought I better try to sleep because who knew what tomorrow would bring. My energy resource was vital to my survival. I had to recharge my batteries.

Morning arrived and I gathered my things, had something to eat, and limbered up. I walked around the graveyard, careful not to step on the burial spots. Maybe I disturbed them last night by not paying attention to where I was walking. I hope they forgive me, I am just a kid. Time to get a move on, so I proceeded, climbing gradually to higher ground, where it was definitely getting colder. I had some long johns in my pack, so quickly slipped them on. Much warmer now, I was ready to meet the weather man. The wind started to blow, and I could feel the bite in the air. Snow was definitely on the way, I hate snow.

An hour later, huge flakes began to cover the ground. I was slipping and sliding everywhere. This was not good, just wasting energy. The flurries did not last long, thank goodness, just long enough to make a mess. The clouds parted and the sun popped through, slowly eating away at the white blanket. I thought the worst was over, and then the earth began to rumble. What was this? What was happening now?

I remembered. The mountain is a volcano and it sounded like it was about to erupt. I tried to see the top, but it was hidden in the clouds. A few minutes later I received my answer. A fiery red glow illuminated the sky and ash began to spew into the atmosphere.

The shaking continued and I could only stand still and hope I would not be sucked into a giant sink hole or devoured by a huge glob of lava. Rocks were starting to sail down the mountainside, large ones, dangerous ones. I had to find a place to hide just in case the mountain really blew its top. Further ahead I saw an opening, amongst the trees, a cave. I ran as fast as I could and entered the darkness. The noise was horrifying, but I felt safer here. I would wait and see what happened. Fireballs careened down the mountainside, one landing in front of the mouth of the cave. Best to go deeper inside I thought.

I felt like I was in the belly of the whale as the mighty mountain shook. The noise, the shaking, and the thought of being melted alive like one of those snowflakes, were terrifying. Farther inside, I kept an eye on the cave entrance, but was beginning to worry.

Large rocks started collecting near the opening and I worried about being trapped inside. It would only take one huge boulder and the exit would be blocked. The rocks were piling up rapidly and I was helpless to stop them. All I could do was watch from the supposed safety of the cave's interior. The rocks and boulders kept coming and the mighty mountain showed no signs of relenting. I was scared, really scared. The entire cave could collapse right on top of me at any time. I would be squashed like a bug, never found in a million years. What a way to go! Not sure what could save me now, only a stroke of luck, or the mountain deciding to take a break and spare me.

The opening of the cave was diminishing, disappearing right before my very eyes as the mountain continued to unleash it fury. Now I could only see a small glimpse of daylight, and then it came. A final barrage of granite crashed down in front of the opening, sealing my fate, entombed in the complete darkness. I was trapped. I could barely see my hands as I held them in front of my face. Now I was shaking along with the mountain. Ten levels beyond terrified, I had to compose myself and think. This was not easy considering my dilemma. I reached into my backpack as I had been given matches and some candles. I located the articles by feel and lit the candle. Moving to the entrance, I began to roll away some of the smaller rocks, but there were huge ones in behind and nothing was going to move those. Maybe this was truly the end of my journey, not the one I had imagined. I stood in shock, staring at the blockade. No way out of this, or was there?

Caves sometimes have dual entrances, sometimes. Clearly I was not going to get out this way and no one would be coming here to look for me. I decided to explore the interior and hope to find the second entrance. I picked up my backpack and made my way through the tunnel. The interior shook for a while longer and then stopped. That in itself was a relief, and the quiet allowed me to concentrate and organize my thoughts. I could smell sulfur, rotten eggs, so gross. I covered my nose, but that didn't help. Get used to it I said. I proceeded, letting the cave lead me into the heart of the mountain, or so I thought. It was creepy and I could only hope the cave was not home to any of the large mountain predators because I had no way to escape.

Deeper in, I began to hear some noise above me. I lifted the candle upwards and could see something moving on the ceiling of the cave. Now the sound of fluttering...bats! I hate bats. They are so ugly and carry diseases like rabies. One bite and I would no doubt suffer a most horrible death. Maybe they were vampire bats and would suck my blood bank dry as a bone? Forget it...they will stay in the darkness and I need to get moving. I kept telling myself there must be another way out, and I was determined to locate it. I pretended to be prospecting for gold, and if I found it, freedom awaited me. I had to do something to take my mind off the severity of the situation. I trudged through the dampness, up and down the rocky sides of the cave, never losing hope, staying confident in my abilities to find the "gold."

I must have walked a mile inside the cave and now could feel a slight breeze. This was a good sign as the fresh air must be coming from outside. I followed the air flow and began to see evidence of increased moisture, then water dripping down the walls. I felt rejuvenated, hopeful I would find my way out. I knew I had been climbing upwards during my trek inside the cave, the incline becoming much steeper as I progressed. My muscles were aching, but now accustomed to the extreme exercise regiment I had been forced to endure over the past few days. My candle was near finished and the breeze was definitely stronger. Up and around a corner I climbed. I looked up and there it was...a small opening.

I was correct...and so fortunate. I could have easily died in here. I moved closer and realized the hole was diminutive, so for me to fit through was going to be a challenge. My clothes were bulky and took up precious space I would need to negotiate my exit. I took off my sweater, removed my backpack and hoped I could now squeeze through. I pulled away some loose impediment and hole was now a little larger. I decided to leave feet first and prayed I didn't get stuck. I lay on my stomach and pushed with my arms. My feet were outside and it was cold. I kept on slowly and my body seemed to fit just right. I wiggled away until my shoulders arrived at the hole. I knew this would be tight. I lowered my right shoulder and tried to maneuver it outside. It was a struggle and very painful, but I forced it through. Success...I did it and now the other was easy. I dragged my sweater and backpack out last and finally I was free.

Facing the small exit, I saluted, slipped my sweater back on and smiled. I placed my backpack over my shoulders and turned around. Yikes! I was on top of a huge glacier. Far below I could make out the line of a narrow pathway. Could that be my path.

I had to get down there...but how? The glacier was not too steep, but was massive and there was no way I could just walk down. The only way was to sit on the ice cap and slowly try to make it down feet first. Easier said then done. I sat on the edge of my backpack to protect my butt from frostbite. I faced the incline and slid along carefully. It seemed to be working until all of a sudden I started to move too fast. I was now butt skiing down a glacier and I had no brakes. I tried to use my heels but at the speed I was travelling I could easily break my ankles, so I just went with it.

I felt like I was going a hundred miles an hour, my eyes were watering like crazy, and the bottom was getting closer, real fast. How would I stop? I could see a wall of snow dead ahead. Maybe it was a wall of ice, I could not tell. If that be the case, I was a dead man for sure. One thing was certain, I was going to hit it and hit it hard. Here we go...hold on...Crash! I plowed into a bank of fresh snow. The speed and force propelled me deep inside the wall. I was buried. Panic set in. I struggled with the weight of the snow, but luckily the compact was of the dry variety so I knew I had a fighting chance. I punched and dug, finally burrowing through the last layer and into the frigid air. Exhausted, I brushed myself off, testing my body parts, all appeared to be intact. I repositioned my backpack and headed for the path leading up the side of the mountain.

A few hours passed and I came to a wooded area heading straight up and then into a clearing of sorts. Standing before me was an unusual formation of stones about three metres high. I could not see in front of me, but the path stopped here. I guess the trail continued on the other side. The Stonehenge-like rocks formed a doorway and the walls continued on for some distance. In fact, I could not see where the walls came to an end.

The formation, resembled some sort of MAZE! I had been to several in my lifetime, but ones made out of hedges and corn stalks. This was more medieval, shaped more like a broken down castle. It was difficult to judge how large or how long, but there was only one way to the other side, through the maze. Reaching the other side did not really concern me. I was worried more about what could be inside. I had to be on high alert, ready for anything.

I cautiously entered the maze. The stones were too high to see over top, so I just followed the corridor for the moment. Soon I had to make a decision...which way to go. From my experience, most mazes made right hand turns, but this was a real puzzle. Built probably hundreds of years ago, the people from that era had their own ideas. I had read many books on mazes, so I hoped my guesses would be accurate. They had to be. If stuck inside this mammoth maze for too long, I would freeze to death.

I motored off to the right and continued to make quick decisions citing the first thing that comes into your mind in usually the correct one. This was not a great time to test this theory, but I was a believer in this thinking process. Usually when you change your mind, you make a mistake or guess wrong. I could not afford any mistakes, not now.

I was determined to solve this giant jigsaw puzzle having little hesitation in moving forward. The width, and the height of the stones varied. Sometimes I could see over the wall, but just saw another wall. The maze was tempting me to try and take a short cut, but I was not falling for that one, certain disaster. The tops of the walls were broken and uneven, so no way to climb along the top of them. Soon I came to an area littered with bones, human bones...skeletal remains. I stopped and wandered what happened here. I heard a grinding sound and hit the deck.

From the other side of the maze, stone projectiles were being hurled at high speed. They bounced off the wall in front of me like buckshot. I crawled out of the area to safety. A booby trap, great. Pay attention I told myself. This is no ordinary maze. Further along I noticed some flat stones on the ground marking the way. I stopped and decided to avoid them, walk around them, and advance through this section. I did so without complication. I had a feeling those stones were there for a sinister reason. I picked up a large stone from the ground and lobbed it onto one of the stepping stones. A huge trap door opened and then shut quickly.

Now I had an idea of what I was up against. This death maze must have been built to torture or kill captured enemies. Maybe it doubled as the purveyor of justice. Suspected criminals may have been given a chance to prove their innocence. If they could arrive at the other end of the maze they would be judged innocent and be freed. If not, it didn't matter. Their fate would be sealed inside the maze.

The labyrinth was very intricate and full of surprises, unpleasant ones. Further along I came to a wall made of one huge flat stone. Carvings of strange animals adorned the surface. The creatures looked like three headed dogs, barking, chasing, and devouring their victims. This ancient artwork instantly provided me an uneasy feeling, my stomach becoming unsettled, not a good sign. The primitive graffiti provided very morbid scene indeed. I sensed I had to garner extra care in this area. I certainly had to watch my step. I tiptoed around trying not to touch the wall or bump into it. The corridor in this part of the maze was extremely narrow and even narrower further up.

My advance was methodical, looking for anything on the ground that may trigger an attack or ambush, booby trap, or otherwise. I turned the corner and came eyeball to eyeball with a mangled, see through corpse floating in mid air. A hologram? Horrified, I screamed at the top of my lungs and the corpse instantly disappeared. I must have been hallucinating.

Suddenly the earth began to shake. Not another eruption? Had my scream caused some sort of avalanche? I looked behind me. The wall containing the drawings of the three headed dogs was vibrating, and it looked like the beasts from hell were trying to push their way through.

My shout, my scream, must have triggered their wanted release. The stone wall now appeared to have become plasticized, allowing the animals to press against the surface. I witnessed bulging shapes trying to push their way through. I watched for several minutes as the dogs attacked the flexible layer of stone. And then it happened. One head, two heads, three heads, finally poked their way through, culminating with a a frenzy of yelping and barking. Time to run, and run fast. The hell hounds' blood curdling, high pitched hysteria was terrifying. Soon they would be free and after me. I was certain they had already picked up my scent. I was the only one in the maze, lucky me. A humongous head start would be needed, or the risk of being ripped to pieces by the gate keepers from Hades would be a fore gone conclusion.

I zigzagged my way through the stone corridors. I could hear the dogs coming and they probably were familiar with every twist and turn, no way to fool or deceive them. Even if I got out they could easily run me down. I kept going, bouncing off the walls as the passageway continued to narrow. If caught in here I would be torn to shreds, merely a blood stain on the stones. Maybe this is where all the others met their untimely fate. The corridor widened up ahead, and I ran for my life. I turned another corner and then another, the maze seemed endless. One more corner and then a huge corridor, an opening, and then...a WALL!

This was too bad to be true. Murphy's Law in the extreme! The stone wall was ten or twelve metres high with no apparent way to scale it. No stairs, no ladder, nothing to use as footings, I was as good as dead. The hounds were advancing posthaste and would arrive within minutes. I rummaged through my backpack and found a rope. Hoping it was long enough, I took it out and tied it around the middle of the blade I had forgotten to return to the leper. I hurled it over the top of the wall hoping the blade would become lodged on something, and I could pull myself up. The first few times failed and I could hear the thundering paws approaching. The canines from hell were too close for comfort, and not much time.

I moved to various areas of the wall and hastily tried again and again. The dogs had arrived. They all stopped short. The throng of blood thirsty beasts stood there panting drooling, and measuring me up. Three sets of black penetrating eyes marking me for death, challenging me to make the first move.

Possessed by the devil, these animals were itching to strike. What were they waiting for? For me to give up? I motioned at them with the blade and they backed up. I tossed the blade over my shoulder, keeping a watchful eye on my attackers. I gently pulled the rope and felt it tighten. I had snagged something. I knew I could not hold the dogs off for long, soon they would have no fear of me, probably didn't now. I made my move. Holding tightly onto the rope, I turned and jumped onto the wall with both feet in a balanced position. The rope seemed secure, but for how long. The dogs went crazy and charged forward in unison to pull me down. I was just out of their reach as they attacked.

The trio jumped up and slammed against the wall trying to climb as I did. I could hear their clawed paws scraping the wall as they slid backwards after each attempt. I prayed the rope would not break or the blade come loose. The fangs of death only a few feet away, I hung on for dear life. No need to look back, the sound of their furry oh so evident. I had to make it up the wall and take my chances from there. The climb was torture, but I kept telling myself I could do this, I had to do this.

I walked the wall, pulling with all my strength. The barking and yelping sent shivers up my spine and the sweat exploded out of my every pore. Near the top, I lunged for the edge grabbing it with one hand and quickly throwing one leg onto the top. I made it...finally. What a godsend...what a relief. I sat their looking down at the crazed animals, still trying to reach me. They wouldn't give up even though I was clearly too high up for them to grab hold of me. I guessed they were hoping I would lose my balance and toppled back into their blood thirsty jaws.

No chance of that, none whatsoever. I held onto the rocky ledge and sneered at the "hellacious" beasts. I still felt uneasy, but knew I had escaped and was safely out of their reach. I looked over my shoulder and saw the most beautiful sight. The summit, I was here, I had made it...it was breath taking. I gazed across the mountain tops, observing nature in all its splendor. I felt calm, peaceful, and relieved. Quiet prevailed, the canine savages had failed. The barking and chaos had ceased. I turned back to look down at the dogs, but they were gone.

I wasn't about to go back down and check out where exactly, I didn't care. I had prevailed. For the moment, I was the king of mountain, the triumphant warrior, winning the battle of all battles, without killing anyone or anything. I was a true survivor. I felt free...truly free.

I stood up on top of the wall and sensed the entire world before me. I was indeed on top of the world. I raised my hands to the heavens and yelled as loud as I could.

"I'm alive! I'm alive! I'm alive."

The cold wind stung my face, and soon the dark clouds disappeared above giving way to the warmth of the sun. I could not move, I was truly amazed and in awe of mother nature and what I had just experienced. I could not believe I was still here. I honestly could not believe it. Then a small shadow passed overhead and I ducked out of instinct. My faithful follower, the blue jay, circled above me and then came to rest on the top of a stone cross at the end of the wall. We looked at each other and the bird chirped uncontrollably. My feathered friend then spread its wings and launched itself from the pedestal high into the sky, disappearing into the sun.

I closed my eyes to calm my mind and realized, to this point in my life, I had achieved nothing. I felt no need to do so, no desire, void of ambition to do anything useful with my life. I was merely floating along in my comfort zone, taking no chance and dong nothing extra to improve myself. In my eyes, I was already good enough. I believed life would take care of me. No need to study hard or apply myself, everything would gravitate towards me because I deserve it, I was already perfect. That's what life is, life is for the taking. Whatever benefited me, or is to my advantage, needed no explanation.

I had been so wrapped in my own little world, paying little or no attention to the world all around me, the real one, the one everybody else lives in. I always had a million excuses for anything and everything, never wrong, taking responsibility for nothing. I was

140

always on the defensive, always reactive, never proactive. Procrastination was my ally, like those who wait until there is only one sheet on the last roll of toilet paper before they go and buy some more. This was me...the real me. The world was my oyster, but I never found the pearl until now. I had it all backwards...everything had to be my way...the wrong way.

Everything has changed now. My thoughts are clear and well defined. I thought about some past events that exemplified my character at the time. I am not proud of my past actions in any way whatsoever, nothing to be proud of, not one single thing.

I have had so many opportunities in my life to prove myself, to improve myself, yet it took an incredible journey to finally prove who I really was, and I don't like what I have discovered. But in all honesty, I am fortunate to have discovered the truth before it is too late. When I think back, I realize I should have done so many things and handled so many situations differently.

I should have defended my schoolmate from Mason the Monster no matter how dire the consequences. After all, he did try and defend me bringing the wrath of the school bully down on himself. I should have hurried to the bus and returned the girl's lost money, it was wrong to keep it.

I should have forgiven my mother for giving away my baseball card collection to charity. Her heart was in the right place. I should have asked for the apples, what is the worst that could have happened? I should have helped the old man and old woman on the escalator. They might have gotten badly injured. The old woman in the stairwell needed assistance, not my uncaring attitude. I should have owned up to kicking the soccer ball through the window. Instead I let someone else take the fall and the ensuing punishment. I should have admitted to what I had done and suffer the consequences. I should have known the handicapped people have a right to go where ever and do whatever they want, just like anyone else, just like I do, no different. They deserve respect, maybe more respect than anyone. I should have not abandoned my friends for personal gain on the playing field or anywhere else, it is just not right. Friends are an important part of anyone's life. Parents are even more important and I must stop taking everything they do for granted. A parent's effort to raise their children is inexhaustible, it never ends. I must realize I owe them everything.

I slowly opened my eyes then began to tremble. I felt a presence somewhere very near, then all around me. Suddenly, all my senses responded to the manifestation and once again, I heard the Voice.

"The lost child has now found his way. The lessons you have learned are more valuable than gold, more valuable than any material wealth, as they will forever guide you along which ever path you choose in life, so choose wisely."

"HONOUR can be considered the "sum-total" of all the previous virtues. One who practices these virtues would surely emerge as an honourable individual. The self esteem and honour of such an individual would be consistently above reproach."

"Reputation, integrity, and moral identity are of the utmost importance to being considered a person of honour. Many cultures consider honour the highest level of human achievement. HONOUR establishes one's credibility, good name, and self worth. HONOUR is understanding your own worth and dignity."

"This virtue is sought after, but only follows the correct behaviour."

The voice faded away just like all the other times

before. I had never paid much attention, too busy trying to survive. This time was different. I really listened and believe I now understood what the Voice was trying to tell me. By reaching the summit I had achieved great honour. I felt a great sense a accomplishment, even though I was not sure exactly what I had accomplished.

I stood alone atop a mountain, but now I was not frightened, and I did not feel lost. The *keys* the Voice had required me to collect were not something of a material nature, not something I could see or hold in my hand. The keys the Voice was talking about last a lifetime and must remain forever ingrained in my mind, heart, and soul. I tried to recollect, even count the number of keys I should have attained. I accounted for nine, but needed ten to find my way. What was the final key? Where could I find it? I thought for awhile. No answers, no ideas, no brainwaves, just another missing piece of this life altering puzzle. How could I return home? Where was the final key that would deliver me there? I had to find it, must be close at hand, I could feel it. Maybe if I stood here long enough, the key would come to me, or was it possible I already had the key and didn't know it. Realizing the final key would not be located on the top of this mountain, I decided to look somewhere else, inside my head, deep inside my mind.

I closed my eyes, raising my arms to the heavens. Almost immediately I experienced a feeling of euphoria. Overcome with calm, I had a feeling this part of my journey had come to an end, it was over. Riding a cushion of air, I floated effortlessly through space and time. I began spinning and tumbling in slow motion. I had no control of what was happening. EVERYTHING WENT BLACK.

TWELVE

The Tenth Key

SUDDENLY EVERYTHING STOPPED. Feeling drowsy, dizzy, and slightly nauseous, I slowly opened my eyes, finding myself at home, seated at my computer desk, gazing out the window at the calming drizzle. I watched the droplets bounce off the pane one by one. The monotonous patter was relentless, somewhat hypnotizing, and I now remember being right here staring out my window. I couldn't recall ever leaving my room, not for a second. Curiously, I turned and checked the clock on the wall. Recalling the approximate time, it appeared the hands had barely moved, maybe a few minutes at most. I had supposedly been gone for days, yet the clock said otherwise. Impossible I thought. Even if I had fallen asleep, the time would have passed as it always does, indicating how long I had been sleeping.

Things just didn't add up. Seemingly no reasonable or logical explanation for what I had experienced, or thought had happened, came immediately to hand. Maybe there wasn't one. How could this be? It all seemed so real, it had to be real...I almost died a hundred deaths. This was a nightmare of epic proportions? A nightmare lasting only a few minutes, but spanning several days? Not sure that was even possible.

Where had I been? What really happened? In the blink of an eye, I had been hurled into a vast wilderness, lost and alone, instructed by a Voice to embark on a mysterious journey. Why me? What was the point? How could it be? Is it possible for time to stand still? Impossible to comprehend, but somehow I knew the experience had been real. I pushed back in my chair and stood, examining my clothes. They were definitely wrinkled and stained with grass, dirt, and sweat. I rolled up my sleeves and pant legs to expose a collection of bruises, scratches, and scrapes. Where did all this come from if I had never left this room? Maybe I fell out of my chair...a hundred times in three minutes. Hard to believe that could be possible, along with everything else.

I began to recollect the exact sequence of events as they were unforgettable, permanently engraved into my subconscious. And the *keys,* what about the *keys?* I remembered the Voice and every single haunting word it spoke. The Voice was trying to tell me something, something important, something I needed to know right now and for the future. Rolling the experience back and forth in my head, I was beginning to put it all together. The message from the Voice was now becoming clear, extremely clear. I believe I had uncovered the answer...as to the keys at least.

The keys were not the kind of keys one would expect to find. I was hoping for keys of gold or keys that would unlock a chest of treasure, not the kind of keys I was presently contemplating. I finally realized I had been collecting the keys every step of the way without even knowing. Piece by piece, I systematically assembled the baffling jigsaw puzzle. The air of confusion was now completely gone. I had the answer. I had the keys. Collecting the keys along the way, I had been oblivious to their meaning or value. I had been expecting something totally different, and was blind to the fact I had been receiving them one by one, each time I was required to make an important decision. If I made the correct choice, I was given the key. Now I understood what was meant by the keys and what the keys really represented.

The first key was COURAGE, the courage I would need to confront any and all difficulties, obstacles, and challenges that lie in front of me, no matter how daunting or intimidating. I would need courage in my life to follow my dreams and succeed in what I hoped to accomplish.

The second key was RECTITUDE, the instinctive ability to do the right thing, make the right decision, knowing the difference between right and wrong and acting accordingly without wavering, void of temptation for personal gain.

The third key was BENEVOLENCE, true goodness of mind, kindness and compassion for others, empathy, understanding, and helping those in need without prejudice.

The fourth key was FORGIVENESS, a truly divine virtue. It takes great courage to forgive. Finding the strength to forgive is indeed difficult, with the greatest difficulty being the ability to forgive oneself.

The fifth key was HONESTY, being truthful in both word and action, truly the law of the Universe. Lying is an act of dishonour and a form of weakness. Tell the truth and take your lumps, you will be a better person for it. The foundation which allows us to perform at our best.

The sixth key was RESPECT, separating us from the animals. Being civilized, having an unbiased consideration for the rights, values, beliefs, and property of others. This conduct spawns courtesy, politeness, etiquette, allowing us to contribute in a positive way to family and society. The "Golden Rule".

The seventh key was LOYALTY, being honest with ourselves and choosing realistic and achievable goals in life. A faithfulness where words and actions are one, no promises necessary, supporting all success.

The eighth key was FILIAL PIETY, unconditional love and respect for one's parents and family lineage. "Honour thy father and thy mother."

The ninth key was HONOUR, the culmination of all the other virtues. Self esteem, reputation, moral identity, and integrity beyond reproach. The highest level of human achievement, credibility and good name. A humble spirit will retain honour.

The Voice noted I must retrieve *TEN KEYS*, before I could find my way. I thought this meant find my way home. This was true in a sense, but actually incorrect. The Voice meant find my way in life. I needed to have all these keys and use them everyday, making them a part of my life. I must not only use them, I must live them. If I did so, I would find myself and find true happiness.

These keys transcend all races, religions, and cultures, interwoven one on top of the other like fabric creating the human dynamic. Life is not about me the "human being", it is about me "being human". The keys are truly the way to happiness and success, but must be used for the benefit of all.

Now I understood the meaning of the first nine keys, but where was the tenth? Where could I possibly find it? I stepped across my room and stood in front of the mirror. I thought I would see nothing, but I did see something...me...a different me. Staring...thinking...staring...thinking, then finally I had it, the location of the tenth key. I knew what the tenth key was. The tenth key was the WISDOM I had obtained along my epic journey. Everything I had experienced and learned was now a part of my life, a very important part. I now had the presence of mind to use the past to shape the future. I now had the wisdom only a very few are privileged to have at such an early age.

Usually, the collection of these keys takes a lifetime, and even then you may only find and use one or two. I now had access to all of them and began to comprehend exactly why. Why me...why was I chosen? The answer to this question was not so complicated. Actually, the answer was all to obvious.

To this point I had learned nothing in my young life, only to take what I could get. I was unyielding, undeniably selfish, and self centered. I listened to no one and was completely uncaring, continually displaying my total disregard for others and their problems. There was only me, myself, and I...the three most important people on this earth. This journey was my wake up call, a warning, an awakening. Now I understand I must change before its too late. That was the message...that is what the voice was trying to tell me.

I tried so hard to write off the Voice's rhetoric as nonsense and a waist of breath that I forgot to listen. I did not want to listen. I had dismissed every single thought about what it takes to become a better person. I didn't care, brushed aside as unimportant, but now, I know I must care and the importance is unquestionable. My new found wisdom will guide me, and I feel confident my future will be full of purpose.

I thought for a moment about wisdom and what it really is. WISDOM is the accumulation of knowledge, experience, teachings, common sense, understanding, and insight, while incorporating the ability to use it.

Sounds so easy, but I know the truth. I remembered a story about a king, a very famous king.

King Solomon, was renowned for his seemingly infinite wisdom. The most documented story is one of two women quarreling over a baby boy, each claiming to be the infant's mother. Solomon decided the appropriate action would be to chop the baby in half, and give half to each woman.

One woman screamed in horror, and pleaded with the king to give the baby to the other woman. Solomon immediately proclaimed, "You are the true mother, as no real mother would allow their child to be severed in two."

With that, Solomon awarded the baby to its rightful mother.

Without doubt, this was the tenth key, and I was determined to use all the keys wisely, determined to live my life in a virtuous manner from this day on.

Success in life is never guaranteed, but at least now I have a sense of what is required. Find yourself and you will find happiness. I hoped this would be true. Even after all this refection and finding out what the keys really meant, many questions still remained. This surely must have been some sort of dream. Time, as we know it, cannot stand still?

I don't believe such can happen, but in this case, my impromptu journey oozed, or at least mirrored reality. Many phenomena cannot be explained, but I was trying my best to convince myself there must be an explanation, a scientific explanation. The laws of physics rule the world, what goes up must come down...right? I remained deeply perplexed and paced around my room a thousand times looking out the window for answers. Now restless, I had to know.

I checked my forehead several times for signs of a fever, which if severe enough can cause hallucinations and delusions. Obviously I had not been in or to the hospital, the clock confirmed so. A car accident, unconscious, or in a coma, the time factor once again reputed the notion. Without doubt, the mystery was real, and one I may never solve. The dream, nightmare theory seemed the only possible scenario, but for some reason I simply could not accept. Exhausted from supposedly doing nothing except sitting at my desk, I walked over to the window, and placed my face against the glass. I could feel the raindrops hit the pane, the vibration like a gentle massage.

I knew my adventure, my experience, my journey, was real, I just knew it. I was convinced, but I was beginning to think I would never be able to prove it. Traumatic events can drive people to the brink of insanity, I hope was wasn't already there.

I backed away and peered out the window. An old woman with a cane and umbrella ambled along the sidewalk in front of my home. She rocked slowly and methodically back and forth like old people do. I did not think much about it until she tilted her umbrella, revealing her face. She turned and I recognized her. It was the old woman I had helped cross the river, who scared the pickpockets, and shunned the leper. I had helped her back to her village and was given a feast fit for a king.

She was dressed differently of course, but I could never forget that face. She smiled, I waved...impossible I thought. She lowered the umbrella to protect herself from the rain and rubbed my eyes in disbelief. In the split second that took, she was gone. At the speed she was walking, she could have not passed my house so quickly. She should still be right there opposite my front door, but she was not.

I had to see for myself, so ran down the stairs and out the front door in an effort to find her. The street was empty, not a soul in sight. I must be seeing things, some sort of mental block or fixation associated with my improbable adventure. Seemed to be happening a lot lately. I ran across the street to the other side trying to catch a glimpse of where she might have gone. None of the neighbours were outside in this weather, so she should be easy to spot. I was hoping to talk to her, to confirm my suspicions. She was nowhere in sight. I threw my hands into the air and dismissed the event sighting fatigue, must be.

I was about cross the street again and return to my room when a car drove slowly up the street passing in front of me. I halted to let the vehicle pass glancing at the occupants. In the passenger's seat was a beautiful young girl. So strikingly gorgeous, a face you could never forget. I knew this girl. I know I had seen her somewhere before, but where? My God! Now I remember, the tribal princess. The most beautiful girl I had ever seen, and there she was, or at least I thought so. I skipped sideways along the walk trying to keep up, trying to secure a better look, trying to confirm the identification.

She looked away and the driver turned to observe my odd behaviour. I thought he may stop the car and say something...that would be great, I would know for sure.

The car did not stop, but I saw something. I noted the driver's unmistakable eyes, dark emerald green...the leper. The car passed too quickly to be certain, then sped up and was soon gone from sight. Standing dumbfounded, my subconscious tweaked because a split second ago I had seen a bag inside the car beside the girl, the colours so familiar. Why would this mille-second flash remain in my mind? I know those colours, school colours, my school colours. Could it be possible? Maybe I was hallucinating from all the events

151

of my chaotic journey? In any event, for the first time in my life, I was genuinely looking forward to attending school come Monday morning.

I crossed the street standing in the rain, soaked from head to toe. I was bewildered beyond belief. What a strange coincidence, or was it? I definitely knew those people. I felt they were now a part of my life. I wondered if I would really ever see them again? I hoped so, seemed apparent, school colours and all, but maybe it was not to be, nothing in life is certain. Time will tell.

Reaching the front door, I stopped on the porch and remembered the princess. Many times she had tried to present me with a token of her appreciation. I declined time after time, but she insisted, and I remember finally accepting. Where did I put the princess' gift? Did I really take it? I became quite excited and dazed at the prospect this event really took place. I knew the chance was slim, the odds astronomical, but I reached into my pocket anyways expecting to find nothing except the usual fluff balls of lint.

Fumbling around I felt something sharp pick my finger...ouch! I removed the object, a splinter from a nut shell, a walnut shell. Where did that come from? Now I was literally shaking. I dove in once again, this time feeling something smooth and round. I pulled it out. There it was...brilliant green jade with a strip of pure gold running through the middle. I remember feeling her soft finger tips as she handed the reward to me.

I rubbed the piece between my thumb and index finger smiling at the sight. This was the proof, enough for me anyways. I had really been there, wherever there was? The keepsake would never leave my possession, a validation of purpose, a constant reminder of what life is really all about. What a great feeling. What a great day. I was ecstatic.

From the treetops I heard a familiar chirping twitter. I looked over my shoulder and there it was, a gorgeous blue jay warbling to the rhythm of the summer rain as the droplets bounced off its evergreen cover.

I smiled and waved to the little bird, after all, he was my best friend. The bluejay had followed me everywhere along my journey. He must have always been somewhere close at hand, like a guardian angel sent from heaven to watch over me.

I raced through the front door, up the stairs, and back into my room. I trotted straight to the window, but the blue jay was gone. Probably felt its job now complete, time to leave me to guide myself. I hoped it would visit often, but if not, I would forever appreciate the pleasure of its company. I realized I had slighted many opportunities and taken what I have, and the people in my life for granted. We come into this world with nothing and leave the same way, without taking anything with us. My life must mean something, and I was determined to make it so. I had indeed found the most valuable treasure of all, and with it I had found myself. I realized my journey had not really ended, but is only just beginning. My life is about to change.

I thought I could finally relax, knowing what I know now, but no such luck. Questions without answers kept niggling away at my peace of mind. Honestly, how could I tell this story to anyone?Would I have to keep this life altering secret hidden inside my inner sanctum for the rest of my life?

The reality is, no one could, or would ever believe me, even if I showed them the stone. The stone would only open up another can of worms. I could inevitably spend the rest of my life defending myself against endless innuendos and accusations because I am the only one who knows the truth. No solution comes to mind. I did not want this experience to continuously torment me, or haunt me. I really want to tell everyone, but how exactly can I do that?

Struggling for hours without resolution, I finally realized there is a way, one way, the only way. I have to write it.

"I"
Quest for the Invisible Keys
Creative Writing Challenge Prizes

First	$ 300 USD	or	£200 Sterling
Second	$ 150 USD	or	£100 Sterling
Third	$ 50 USD	or	£30 Sterling

Creative Writing Challenge

At the end of the story, the child notices the clock on his room wall has only counted off two or three minutes, but the child recalls being gone for several days. What is your theory? Explain the time lapse in 250 words or less. Your creative imagination is the "invisible key" to this puzzle.

Each entry must be forwarded with the proof of purchase.

One entry per each proof of purchase.

Name – Age – City of Residence – E-mail - must be included on the front your submission. Forward via e-mail as MS Word or Rich Text Format attachment to contact@gstuartnakay.com

All entrants will automatically be enrolled free in "Evolution X", a club where imagination has no limitations.

Winning submissions will be published online for all to enjoy at www.gstuartnakay.com

Deadline is October 31, 2012
Prizes awarded on December 31, 2012.